THE
PERILOUS
PARAKEET

BY

L.G. CUNNINGHAM

JITTERS

ISBN-13: 9781697101508

DEDICATION

To Cinta & Barney – for introducing me to the world of horror and scary stories at a most unsuitable age!

CONTENTS

Chapter 1 1

Chapter 2 5

Chapter 3 10

Chapter 4 16

Chapter 5 22

Chapter 6 28

Chapter 7 33

Chapter 8 39

Chapter 9 44

Chapter 10 50

Chapter 11 55

Chapter 12 61

Chapter 13 66

Chapter 14 70

Chapter 15 76

Chapter 16 80

Chapter 17 86

Chapter 18 91

Chapter 19 95

Chapter 20 100

Chapter 21 106

Chapter 22 112

Chapter 23 117

Chapter 24 123

Chapter 25 128

Chapter 26 133

Chapter 27 139

Chapter 28 144

Chapter 29 148

Chapter 30.. 154

Chapter 31.. 160

About the Author.. 166

The hairy tarantula skittered unnaturally fast on its eight legs, sinking its sharp fangs deep into the helpless cricket.

"Muahahaha," I cackled in my most evil, super-villainous voice. I get great enjoyment out of feeding Matilda. It's so much more exciting than feeding the tropical fish those smelly flakes or feeding the rabbits lettuce! Although, she only needs to eat like twice per week, so I try to make the most out of the occasion.

Matilda is one of the many pets we keep in our backyard zoo. Now, when I say backyard zoo, you're probably thinking of a huge area with enclosures and zookeepers and hippos – whereas it's more of a large garage converted to house a couple of exotic and not so exotic animals.

"Archie, Dad said it's time to go. Eugh! That's totally disgusting!"

That's my eleven-year-old sister, Sophia – a human tornado. We're nothing alike. She hates animals. I love them. She's annoying. I'm not. See where I'm going with this?

I'm also a full year older than her but you would swear she was the one on the verge of becoming a teenager. All she does is hang around the mall with her troupe of cackling friends, giggling about stuff only girls understand... and her head is forever stuck in her phone!

It really bugs me when people say we look alike. Yes, we both have flaming red hair and faces full of freckles. But she wears her hair straight and always in a ponytail. My hair is short and impossibly curly. Everyone calls her '*cute as a button*', what with her wide blue eyes and long eyelashes. Nobody calls me cute! They call me shrimpy four eyes – yes, I have round glasses that sit on a long nose that, apparently, I got from my Dad's side of the family – but I'm sure that will change when I get my growth spurt... any day now...

"Here Sophia, there's plenty to go around," I said, picking up a live cricket and holding it in her direction.

"You're sick, Archie. You know, you really have to get a new hobby? Something that involves interactions with *actual* people, and by people, I mean the two-legged type? No fur, no fangs... just normal regular people!"

I tried to think of a clever response, something that would put my know-it-all sister right back in her place but I came up short. Like I always did when it came to competing with the golden child. So, I wound my arm back, fully planning on using the would-be spider dinner as a chirping missile, when the garage door banged open.

"Archie, Sophia, there you are! I was wondering where – wait, what's going on here?"

"Good question, Dad. Archie what were you about to do?" Sophia said, smirking.

"Erm... nothing going on here, Dad," my arm was still poised in a throwing position, "just feeding our animal friends here and practicing my throws for the big dodgeball game."

Not a bad cover story in my opinion. It might have held up only for the cricket in my hand decided to chirp at that very moment. Great timing. Spectacular.

Thankfully, Dad brushed over the whole scene and said, "Well let's get a move on! I hope you both haven't forgot its Sunday afternoon which means…"

Sophia groaned loudly.

"Sunday family adventures!" I shouted gleefully.

"That's right, my boy! And I know you're both just going to love what I have planned for today!"

I love Sunday afternoons. Every Sunday for as long back as I can remember, Dad brings us on a family trip to somewhere new and exciting. Well I found the trips exciting anyway.

"Oh, please don't say it's a behind the scenes tour of the zoo again!" Sophia cried.

Dad pulled his pants higher up over his round waist. He was always fidgeting with his belt or pants, as if he could never get a pair that fit him properly.

Wait, did I mention my Dad is a zookeeper? I think he's the coolest Dad in the world. I definitely got my love of animals from him. One day I plan to follow in his footsteps. Head Zookeeper Archie Jones. Has a nice ring to it, doesn't it? Maybe I'd also discover a new species and go down in history. Or prevent the extinction of an endangered animal? Anyway, enough about my dreams.

"Not today Soph, we had a nasty incident in the gorilla enclosure that I won't get into but believe me when I say I need a break from the place until at least tomorrow!" He wiped his head with the back of his hand.

Sophia had already lost interest in the conversation and was obnoxiously tapping away on her phone. I remember when she used to love our Sunday excursions. Now she was just *too cool* and grown up for them.

"Now, get your coats and we shall hit the road. And Archie, make sure every cage is closed tightly. And I mean *every* cage. We don't want a repeat of last Sunday!"

I don't want to get into what happened last Sunday. Let's just say it involved a snake, a Sunday roast and a lot of screaming from my mom and sister.

"You can count on me, Dad, won't happen again. No more accidents – I promise!" I said confidently, saluting like I was an army sergeant.

I don't like breaking promises. But in fairness, I can't foresee the future. I had no way of knowing that I had just made a promise that I couldn't keep. Last Sunday's mishap would look like a drop of spilled milk compared to the *accidents* I was about to get into.

"Did you know that a rhinoceros' horn is made of hair? Or that slugs have four noses? I bet you never knew that almost three percent of the ice in the Antarctic is penguin urine!"

I was reading from a graphic manual I picked up in the library recently, 101 FACTS YOU DON'T KNOW ABOUT ANIMALS, as the maroon SUV drifted over newly tarmacked roads.

"No, I didn't know that, Archie, and this may sound surprising to you, but guess what? No-one cares about penguin pee facts!" Sophia said from the front seat.

"Kids, no toilet-related talk in the car please. Can't we just enjoy each other's company for the afternoon with no fighting?" Dad asked.

Sighing, I rested my chin in the palm of my hand and looked out of the window at our boring neighbourhood. I say boring, because nothing exciting or out of the ordinary has ever happened in my twelve years of living on this block. In fact, the same can be said for the whole town of Virginia Falls. The most exciting thing to happen recently was when a kid was reported missing by a young worrisome couple. The town was turned upside down in the search for the girl, only for her to appear downstairs, yawning and wondering why mommy and daddy were so upset. You see, the distraught parents neglected to thoroughly check their child's bedroom, specifically the wardrobe where she lay sleeping soundly while Virginia Falls panicked. Bad things just didn't happen in the area, so naturally people turned into nervous nellies at the first sign of potential trouble.

We passed by red-bricked detached and semi-detached houses, green grass glittering from their perfectly mowed lawns. Golden rays of afternoon spring sunlight broke through the tall surrounding trees that lined the sidewalks. Spotlights of sunshine dotted the roads. It was like somebody was shining a giant torch through the gaps in the trees.

"So Dad, where are you taking us today? Is it the Weird and Wonderful Museum?" I asked excitedly. "Oh, I bet that's where we're going! Come on, Dad, I'm dying to know!"

"You would fit in perfectly at that museum Arch... in the *weird* section anyway," Sophia quipped, head still buried in her phone.

Dad frowned in her direction and then looked into the rear-view mirror so he could see me clearly. He smiled and said, "Ah, I don't want to spoil the surprise. Trust me when I say you will love it!"

Sophia grunted from the front seat or maybe she tut-tutted in disapproval – I wasn't sure which, but I knew she wasn't as excited as I was for this Sunday's adventure.

"Arch, you sound like such a dork! Dad just tell us

where we're going... we're not kids anymore, you know."

I could see a pained look cross Dad's face momentarily. It was perhaps a look of acknowledgement that his kids were no longer excited by typical kid things such as Sunday adventures, ice-cream sandwiches or family picnics.

Not me. I still love all those things! Especially ice-cream sandwiches!

"Patience is a virtue sought by many but found by few, darling," Dad said.

I knew this confused Sophia as she looked sideways quizzingly, so I added, "It means you should stop acting so spoilt for once in your life. Oh, and also that you have the patience of a new-born puppy waiting to get fed."

That's not exactly what it meant if I'm totally honest. But my sister was annoying me even more than usual, so I wanted to put her in her place. And oh boy, did it work.

Tantrum time.

Her face started to turn beetroot red. Any second now she would unleash a shrill wail that would shake the very foundations of the SUV. She opened her pursed lips, inhaled deeply and—

"We're going to an animal sanctuary!" Dad interrupted, right on queue.

Phew! I lowered my hands from the sides of my head. My ear drums were safe for another day.

"Another Sunday trip to a pet store? Very original, Dad!" Sophia said sarcastically.

Dad ignored Sophia and continued, "I first heard about it from this new guy who volunteers at weekends in the zoo. He turned up two months ago out of nowhere offering to clean the enclosures, which is just fine by me! Actually, I'm pretty sure he doesn't even get paid? Anyway, he mentioned there was a safe haven for animals on the outskirts of town. Near Clarkes forest. And it's open to the public!"

As Dad finished, the SUV left the leafy neighbourhoods behind and rolled into a vast expanse of countryside. Tightly knit red-bricked homes were replaced with rolling hills, dotted with isolated dwellings. We passed under a large billboard sign that read: VIRGINIA FALLS WILL MISS YOU - COME BACK SOON!

"Bor-ing!" Sophia said, tapping the screen of her phone in frustration at whatever app she was playing.

Probably some dumb *candy crush* game.

"Maybe you wouldn't be so bored if you spent less time playing those dumb games and interacted with me and Dad?"

"*I* won't interact with anyone? Archie, when was the last time you brought a friend over to our house? Huh? And by *friend,* I mean a *human* friend, not a four legged one."

"Now kids that's enough! Please. Don't make me turn this car around," Dad said tiredly.

It took a lot of willpower but I decided not to engage with my sister, even though her words stung me bitterly. True, it had been a long time since I had a friend over to the house. The last time didn't end so well and that story had spread around school like ants on a picnic. Think Matilda and think accidental open cage and you will get the idea.

"We're almost there kids," Dad informed us happily. "It's just past Clarkes forest, up here on the right. Now keep your eyes peeled, the new guy did tell me the entrance is difficult to spot—"

"Owwww HELP! Dad, HELP ME!" Sophia cried suddenly. Her eyes went wide and fearful. She started to jerk uncontrollably in the front seat.

Dad looked worryingly at Sophia while trying to concentrate on the road.

"What's wrong, sweetie? What is it?"

He pulled the car abruptly to the right, off the main road, narrowly avoiding an oncoming truck that roared past.

"Something is... is... BITING MY LEG!" she screamed.

Sophia continued to thrash up and down wildly in the front – kind of how I would imagine someone to behave if they had a colony of ants down their pants.

The SUV's hazard warning lights flashed and ticked on the side of the road as Dad looked on helplessly, unsure what to do to help.

I, on the other hand, was failing miserably to contain the giggles. Tears of laughter formed at the corners of my eyes.

Sophia stopped shrieking like a baboon and reached down to her ankle.

"ARCHIE!" she shouted angrily. "I told you to keep Lizzie away from me!"

Clasped in her hand was my yellow, white and black spotted best friend, Lizzie. We have been together for as long as I can remember. I think it was a first birthday present from Dad. She's a leopard gecko (hence the black spots), about eight inches long and is surprisingly active and excitable for a lizard. I take her everywhere with me. She also lives in my room in a large tank which is pretty cool.

I never feel alone when Lizzie is around.

"Calm down, Sophia, Lizzie wouldn't hurt a fly," I said, wiping away the tears with one hand and grabbing my lizard with the other.

"Lizzie *eats* flies!" Sophia retorted. Her body was still shaking.

I didn't see what the big deal was?

"Son, please don't set your lizard on your sister. Your mother and I discussed this at your last PTA. You shouldn't be bringing Lizzie outside the house with you," Dad scolded as he waited for the oncoming traffic to pass before pulling the car back onto the main road.

"Sorry Dad; won't happen again," I promised.

We drove in silence for another two minutes before Clarkes forest came into view. I forgot how big it is! We use to have family picnics out here. It reminded me of a vast furry green carpet or like a field of broccoli heads bunched together. I shuddered thinking about how easy it would be to get lost in there. I also shuddered at the thought of broccoli.

"Keep your eyes peeled guys, must be somewhere here," Dad said hopefully.

A large shack-like dwelling came into view as we rounded a corner. It was partially hidden on a lone dirt road, surrounded by the thick forest.

Dad looked around uncertainly and said, "This must be the place, I can't see anything else out this way."

We veered off the road, coming to a stop on a dirt path that ended near the entrance to our presumed destination.

I made sure Lizzie was tucked away comfortably in my pocket before stepping out of the car.

It was a crisp Sunday, fresh but cold enough for us to bring our heavy winter coats. I immediately noticed the sharp, sweet, refreshing smell of the surrounding pine trees.

If nature had a smell, this was it.

"Alrighty, let's go check this place out," Dad said as he buttoned up his jacket.

The closer we walked to the building, the larger the shadows grew. The late spring afternoon sunlight struggled to get through the density of the trees and branches.

"This is too creepy. What if a murderer lives in here?" Sophia said.

"Don't be silly darling, there aren't any murderers in Virginia Falls. You're watching too many scary movies."

The first thing that struck me as strange was the distinct lack of signposts or signage. It was as if this place didn't want visitors. As if, it wanted to be left alone.

Secondly, the dwelling looked like it had been abandoned a long time ago. The two windows to the front were shuttered closed.

Dad stepped onto the porch and rapped the rotted wooden door loudly.

"Hello? Anyone home?"

When nobody answered, he pushed the door gently open and peered inside.

A wide smile spread across his round face.

"This is the place kids, go in and see for yourselves."

"No way am I going in there," Sophia said, crossing her arms over her chest.

Of course, she had to act up. I didn't expect any less.

I brushed past her, entering through the corroded door – and stopped in amazement.

Dad was right, this was the place. A motley of cages hung from the ceiling, containing many colourful species of bird who chirped and squawked. Dogs of all shapes and sizes sat, slept, yapped and paced in their spacious pens. Brilliant ocean blue fluorescent light shone from the aquarium in the rear of the room as tropical fish swam quietly to and fro. Bizarrely, I even spotted an elderly chimpanzee resting on a branch in the room's largest enclosure. On top of all of this, there were hamsters, meerkats, rabbits, turtles and much much more.

I was in heaven.

"IT STINKS IN HERE," Sophia shouted above the racket.

She wasn't lying, when you walked in the smell hit you like a punch in the face. You know the smell you get when you walk into a pet store? Wet dog mixed with a variety of animal poop? Yes, that stench.

Call me weird but I kind of like it! I am well used to these smells anyway. Our backyard zoo doesn't exactly smell of lavender.

While Dad worked on convincing Sophia to

remain inside, I wandered off aimlessly. My eyes lit up at how peculiar and marvellous this place was. It was nothing more than a large rundown wooden shack but my eyes saw past such superficial details.

The old chimpanzee stared at me through dark brown, suspicious eyes as I ambled through the centre of the sanctuary.

I took a right turn, past a cage of fluffy black and white kittens miaowing for my attention, and spotted a poster that read 'Reptile Haven'.

Yes! Given that my best friend is a gecko lizard, you won't be surprised to learn that I find reptiles very interesting. Did you know that nearly all reptiles are cold blooded? And that the first reptiles are almost three hundred and twenty million years old? Cool, right? Anyway…

Before I could properly examine the reptile collection, a low menacing growl stopped me in my tracks. Coming from somewhere to the left. I slowly turned my head in the direction of the ominous sound.

"*Yikes!*" I mumbled silently when I discovered the source of the growl. A huge grey and white wolf had strolled around the corner and to its obvious delight, had just discovered its next meal… *me*!

"*Grrrrrrrrrrr.*"

"D-D-Dad," I tried to call for help but I could only croak above a whisper. My throat was so dry. My whole body froze. I felt paralysed, too terrified to make any sudden movements.

Why isn't this wolf locked up? How did it escape? Many questions ran through my mind but none of them were going to help me now. I tried to will my body to move, to step away from the danger I was in but it was no use – my limbs had given up.

The wolf must have sensed my intentions because it took one step towards me.

Two steps.

Three.

Fangs bared in an angry snarl, foam dripping from blood red lips, the hungry wolf leaped at me.

I closed my eyes, waiting for the inevitable clamp of its jaws around my throat. Waiting for it to end my life.

The next three seconds felt more like three hours. As I waited for the excruciating pain of the wolf's fangs on my flesh, I thought of all the things I would never get to do in life. Like explore the jungles of Borneo. Safari in the Kruger National Park. Become a zookeeper like my Dad. Or own a penguin.

Eyes still closed, body shaking like a leaf, I slowly pried one eye open. I didn't know how I was still breathing. Or maybe, I had died and just not realised it yet?

When the room came into focus, I was surprised to see the wolf cradled in the arms of a tall and very peculiar man.

"Children shouldn't wander around alone, one could get hurt," he said in a raspy voice.

The man wore an outlandish dark maroon robe. Something like a wizard might wear. He had an egg-shaped skull, completely bald other than a black greasy ponytail on the back of his head. It reminded me of a horse's tail. His dark eyebrows were pointed downwards in an endless frown above a narrow set of cold eyes. Cold and unkind.

I shirked under the intensity of his gaze.

"Your wolf nearly ate me," I managed to say. I was still shaking all over.

"Wolf? You mean this harmless creature?" He gestured at the huge shape resting in his arms, "No child, this canine is a crossbreed between two wolf-like species. A Siberian Husky and German Shepherd. While it may resemble a wolf in appearance, its genetic code says otherwise. And therefore, you have nothing to fear." He smiled crookedly, fixing me with a hard stare, as if I had done something wrong.

I wasn't the one who let wolf-like dogs loose around the general public! Snakes and spiders maybe... but never a wolf!

Just when the silence was turning uncomfortable, Dad and Sophia appeared behind me.

It looked like Dad had to physically drag Sophia to get her to this point. He had a hold of one wrist as she tugged in the other direction. Her other hand covered her nose and mouth. The natural smells of the animal kingdom were not her cup of tea.

"Ah, Mr Schimmel, is it?" Dad said to the creepy man. "Your shelter is mightily impressive—"

"Shelter? What you see before you is more than just a shelter," Mr Schimmel said in an offensive tone. "This is a haven, offering liberation from the cruelties of the world we live in. My sanctuary offers a second chance at a better life to these poor unfortunate creatures who were deemed unworthy by their owners. Unloved and uncared for. Some have even suffered levels of abuse that justify a life sentence behind bars."

He paused momentarily and placed the now docile

wolf-dog on the dirt ground. The previously ferocious hound rubbed its large head against Mr Schimmel's leg affectionately before trodding off in the opposite direction. Its tail wagged happily as it disappeared around a corner.

That was strange, I thought to myself. *A minute ago, that wolf-dog was about to turn me into dog chow!*

I felt something move against my thigh. I reached into my pocket and gently caressed Lizzie. Her scales felt rough and leathery.

She probably sensed my fear.

We always had that kind of a connection. Much like how I would imagine it is with twins. Only, Lizzie and I aren't twins... obviously.

Mr Schimmel gestured towards the many surrounding animals before continuing, "So you see, this is no mere shelter. Nor a zoo for your entertainment," at the mention of zoo, Dad's rosy cheeks turned a bright shade of pink, "or a pet store for you to ogle at the goods on sale."

"Ah yes, my apologies," Dad said. "I meant no disrespect towards your, erm, sanctuary. I'll grab my family and we will be out of your hair."

"Indeed," Mr Schimmel added, unsmiling.

It was crystal clear that this guy wanted us gone. And to be honest, I was only happy to oblige. A sense of unease had been growing on me. Maybe it had to do with the near-death experience, or the creepy Mr Schimmel, but there was something about this place that just didn't sit right with me.

"Sophia?" Dad called. "Sophia? Time to go, sweetie.

Where are you?"

Sophia was no longer behind Dad; she must have slipped away during the awkward stand-off.

I followed Dad to what was the foyer of the shabby building. We passed a large tank that was home to an angry-looking snapping turtle. The old chimp continued its solemn gaze at us as it swung back and forward on a tyre.

We found Sophia leaning against a desktop, admiring what looked like an antique birdcage. As I stepped closer, I noticed the impressive design of the cage. Red and gold spirals criss-crossed on the main frame. Intricate symbols were carved into the base, just above the legs. It was definitely hand crafted.

And it was occupied.

Inside, perched on a cotton rope was a little yellow parakeet. It looked about six inches long with beautiful golden plumage. It had beady black eyes and an area of tough blue skin above its beak that was striking against the all-yellow feathers.

Sophia was in love. She eyed the tiny bird longingly.

"There you are, time to go, we don't want to be late for dinner."

Sophia kept her stare fixed on the parakeet. "Dad, I want this bird. Please, please, please!"

"Sweetie this isn't a pet store, we can't just take what we want," Dad said uncomfortably.

"Correct Mr Jones," Mr Schimmel had appeared quietly behind us, "this is no puppy farm, I hope you can educate your children on—"

He didn't finish his sentence. He had a strange look on his face. I wasn't sure what was going on but I had a hunch that he was surprised to see the birdcage as he was gazing at it suspiciously. As if it wasn't supposed to be there.

"Curious…" he said.

"Sorry, what is?" Dad asked, clearly as confused as I was.

"You see, Mr Jones, some of my companions find me in ways I cannot explain. Perhaps my sanctuary calls to them, speaks to their animal senses." His eyes took on a faraway look.

"Dad, I want the parakeet," Sophia said, hopping up and down on the spot with excitement.

I tugged at Dad's coat. "Dad, let's just get out of here, I don't like this place."

"Soph, like Mr Schimmel said, you can't take the bird home—"

"Perhaps in this instance," Mr Schimmel interrupted, "I can part ways with this creature. After all, Mr Jones, you do care for animals for a living, yes?"

"How did you know?"

"Judging by your nametag and Virginia Falls Zoo sweater I somehow reached that complex conclusion."

"Oh, right," Dad's face turned an even deeper shade of pink.

"I promise I'll take good care of her. I'll feed her, sing to her, play with her and even clean her cage," Sophia pleaded.

"Archie, are you OK with this too? You will need

to help your sister find a nice spot for the bird at home?"

"What? Oh yeah, sure, whatever... let's just go," I said, fixing my glasses on my nose. I was so eager to be out of this place I wouldn't have noticed if Dad said we were taking the old chimp home.

Mr Schimmel stroked his goatee, as if deep in thought. Finally, he said, "Take the bird, but note this, my friends here are for life. I do not part with them easily. By taking one home, you're entering a bond with another living creature which cannot be broken. A girl or boy's relationship with their animal is sacred. Do you understand?"

"Yes sir, I do. Thank you, thank you, thank you!" Sophia cried excitedly.

Sophia grabbed the antique birdcage and ran out of the building. Dad thanked Mr Schimmel one final time before waddling out after her.

I followed them both, keen to be away from the place. I took one last look over my shoulder.

Mr Schimmel was staring directly at me.

Os' of smoke sailed to the ceiling from a pipe held between his lips. The corners of his mouth curled into an evil smirk.

I checked that Lizzie was still safely in my pocket and swiftly exited Schimmel's sanctuary.

"Did you know a parakeet's heart beats over 300 times per minute? And they can have up to three thousand feathers on their body... amazing!" Dad said matter of factly.

"I wonder what I'll call her. Actually, is it a girl or a boy? I hope it's a girl," Sophia added.

The journey back home continued much like this. I didn't feel the need to inform her that it was a male parakeet. I knew this because the blue area above the beak was typically blue on males and brown on females.

I sat silently, looking out of the window at nothing in particular. The sun was making its final descent beyond the horizon as we crossed the line back into Virginia Falls. Shadows were starting to creep out as the afternoon passed into evening.

I did try to explain to Dad that I had nearly been torn apart by the giant dog but he just laughed at me. Apparently, I got spooked due to the *size* of the dog. Apparently, it just wanted some *attention*.

Yeah, right... attention. It wanted me for dinner and it almost got its wish!

I also couldn't understand how he didn't find it strange or one bit weird that Mr Schimmel suddenly decided to let us take the bird home? He made it clear it wasn't a pet store and yet here I was sitting in the backseat beside the birdcage which was covered by a musty blanket Dad found in the trunk of the SUV.

It was Dad's idea to cover the cage with a blanket. He thought the bird would be spooked in the car and that it would be calmer in the dark. It hadn't made a sound since we departed the strange sanctuary so I suppose he knew what he was talking about.

Dad glanced at his wrist nervously as the SUV entered our leafy, uneventful neighbourhood.

"Kids, we're going to tell your mother we got stuck in a major traffic jam on the way home."

"But Dad, are you asking us to lie to Mom?" Sophia said incredulously. "But you always tell us to be truthful and that lies are hurtful?"

Yeah right! As if she had never told a lie! Only last week during her birthday party she had successfully pinned the blame on me for the smudged birthday cake on the living room walls.

I didn't leave my room. Not even to get a slice of cake. It wasn't worth entering the war zone of screaming ten-year-old girls. Not even for chocolate cake dripping with melted raspberry frosting.

My parents always fell for her innocent, puppy dog, watery eyes act. I can cross my eyes but that's about it.

"Errr... yes, Soph, I do but... this is only a *white* lie.

It's a variation of the truth that's in everyone's best interests. Especially mine... I can't have us late for another dinner and not have a good excuse!" Dad said as he squirmed in his seat.

I chuckled at my Dad's discomfort as we pulled into the asphalt driveway of our red-bricked home.

The porch light flicked on.

Mom was leaning against the front door, arms crossed, eyebrows raised questioningly. She was a tall woman, especially when compared to Dad. Where he was round and stumpy, she was tall and skinny as a stick insect. Fair blond curly hair tumbled against her nurses' uniform.

It wasn't a good idea to get on the wrong side of Mom. She could be quite terrifying when she was in a bad mood. You should have seen her when she slipped on our rabbit Arnold's droppings in the backyard. Like a crocodile with a toothache!

"Hello dear, fine spring evening isn't it?" Dad said as he waddled out of the SUV.

"Don't *dear* me, Robert, the dinner is sitting on the table going cold and I'm on the night shift this evening. What took you so long?"

"Well, you see... really bad traffic jam—"

"Mom come meet our new family member, she's just the prettiest little thing," Sophia interrupted. She yanked the birdcage out of the backseat and half-sprinted, half-dragged it into the house. She grabbed Mom by the hand and led her away from the door.

Dad and I looked at each other and shrugged our shoulders.

"Well at least that changed the subject," he said cheerily.

We left the chilly dark evening behind and walked into the cosy warmth of the living room. Fragrant spices filled the air which could only mean one thing – it was *spag bol* night.

My tummy rumbled. No-one could make Bolognese quite like my Mom.

"Arch, after you hang your coat up, I want you to take Soph's bird out to the garage. Find a nice place for it. Then wash your hands and join us for dinner," Mom declared briskly.

"Why do I have to take *Sophia's* pet out to the garage?"

I glanced at Sophia who was sprawled on the living room carpet, ripping open presents. Probably just arrived from Grandma. She had forgotten about her new favourite pet already.

At the look on Mom's face, I decided it wasn't a good time to argue.

"Fine," I said, sighing loudly. I grabbed the large bird cage under one arm and exited the living room.

"It's not been our day, has it Lizzie?" I said to the lizard who poked its head out of my pocket for a look. "Actually, it hasn't been a good week—"

Something fast and small darted across my path, causing me to lose my balance and crash to the laminated floor. My glasses flew off my nose.

"Owww, that's going to bruise in the morning," I said, holding my knee. "Buster! Be careful next time, I could have stood on you!"

Buster is our family dog, a black and tan coated King Charles. He is the only animal we're allowed to keep in the house. Mom fell in love with him ever since he arrived at our doorstep a couple of weeks ago. We put some ads in the paper but nobody called to claim him so I guess he is staying with us for good.

Buster barked once and ran into the living room.

The garage, or 'backyard zoo' as I like to call it, looks like your typical garage that at first glance should store only a lawn mower, power tools and other garden related items. But inside, it is like our own version of an animal sanctuary—without scary wolf dogs of course. We have a rabbit (Arnold), three hamsters (Jim, Joe & Bob), a snake (Trevor), some tropical fish (who I didn't bother to name) and a tarantula (who of course you know as Matilda). I plan to keep adding to our animal family but I certainly didn't plan for a parakeet to be the newest member.

I placed the bird cage on an old paint-chipped desk, in front of our fish tank.

"Well, this bird's a part of the family whether we like it or not, Lizzie. Suppose we will feed it when Sophia forgets. Which will probably be every day."

I was just about to leave and wash up for dinner when I realised the blanket was still covering the cage.

"Better remove this and let the new guy see his new home," I said aloud.

As soon as I dropped the blanket to the floor, something odd happened with the other animals. Arnold started running in circles wildly, rustling the straw in his cage. Trevor, who doesn't move very much, was slithering around in his tank. Matilda reared on her two rear-most legs, as if preparing to attack. Jim, Joe & Bob all crammed in to the hamster wheel.

Chirp.

Silence. The garage's inhabitants stopped moving immediately.

That's weird, I thought.

Confused, I looked at the golden bird who peered back. My imagination was definitely running away from me today.

Turning on my heel, I made to exit the garage.

Chirp.

I looked back again and for a split second, I could have sworn the black eyes of the bird glowed a fiery red.

We sat around the mahogany table for dinner, just like we did every night. I devoured my first helping of Mom's famous Bolognese and was now tucking into my second.

"Soph, wipe your mouth please, where is your manners?" Mom said. "You're getting more food on your face than into your mouth."

Sophia slurped her spaghetti noisily. She always chews her food loudly on purpose, mouth wide open, just to vex me.

"As I was saying, I'm off to San Francisco to assist with the transportation of a red panda. Very important business. The boss reckons it will draw in some big crowds. He confides a lot in me lately. Pretty soon I'll be promoted to head zookeeper and then I'll get the respect I deserve, dear. It's only a matter of time for Robert Jones!" he said proudly.

Dad was sipping from a coffee mug, the daily newspaper hiding his face from view. My eyes were briefly drawn to the headline plastered on the front page: 'LOCK UP YOUR PETS - CRAZED LUNATIC FLEES WESTLAKE FOR ANIMAL MALPRACTICE.'

"Of course you will, Robert. Good things come to those who wait. Arch – are you excited for your dodgeball match this Tuesday?" Mom said, changing the subject and drawing my attention away from the newspaper.

What Mom was referring to was the school's national dodgeball qualifier match. Only two days away.

Dodgeball. I bloody hate dodgeball. How could anyone enjoy getting pelted with a heavy ball? If I had my way, I would be playing no dodgeball. Unfortunately for me, I didn't have that luxury. Coach Harrison, the red-faced, always angry P.E. teacher, had promised to flunk me unless I took part in a school team sport. Somehow, I ended up on the dodgeball team. My school, Montgomery Elementary, had a real chance of reaching the nationals this year. I feel sick thinking about it.

To make matters worse, the rest of the team were not one bit happy with my inclusion. As the kid who was always picked last for school sports, I wasn't exactly a strong addition to the team.

"You know I'm not, Mom. But I have no choice. If I don't play, I'll flunk P.E. If I do play, I'll cost the team the game. Win-win situation for me," I said sarcastically.

"Practice makes perfect, my boy," Dad said cheerily.

"I don't have the time to practice, Dad. Between school projects, homework and taking care of the zoo out the back, my schedule just wouldn't allow it," I said between a mouthful of meatballs.

"Maybe you should spend less time with freaks like that new caretaker," Sophia shot back.

"Sophia, less of that please," Mom said.

I glared at my sister across the table. She stuck out her tongue at me.

"Are you happy with your new bird, Soph?" Mom asked. "I hope you're going to take extra special care of it."

I snorted into my food.

"Yes Mom, I love her! She's so pretty with her yellow feathers and tiny beak. I'll clean her and feed her every day."

Sure she would.

Another promise she wouldn't keep. Just like the promise to walk Buster every day. I bet she didn't even know where his lead was!

"Let me get this straight, you're going to go out to the garage *every* day? The one place at home you refuse to enter. You're going to clean the cage, feed the bird and you won't mind doing all of this beside the other animals?"

"Yes, *Archie*, didn't you just hear what I said? I'm going to take great care of her."

"Her?" I couldn't resist. "You know it's a boy."

"NO!" she screamed. "Mom, Dad, tell him it's a girl."

"OK who wants birthday cake?" Mom said, once again changing the subject. "Grandma sent you a cake with her presents, Soph. Aren't you very lucky to have such a thoughtful grandmother?"

She was super spoilt. Her second cake in a week!

Her face lit up at the mention of cake, immediately forgetting all about our argument. I helped Dad clear the table while Mom brought in the fresh cream sponge, dripping in raspberry sauce and dotted with fresh strawberries.

I looked at the stack of sugary goodness hungrily. There was always room for cake.

Maybe Lizzie would like a taste? I reached down into my pocket and was alarmed to find that it was empty.

Sophia grabbed the carving knife from the table and moved toward the cake. She brought the knife down—and screamed at the top of her lungs.

"Mom! That disgusting *lizard* is in the middle of my CAKE!"

I looked closer and sure enough, there was Lizzie's head poking from the middle of the cake, cream icing giving her a white beard. She must have burrowed her way in, like a tiny mole.

How she got there, I had no idea. But I knew enough to know that I wouldn't be sampling the scrumptious icing tonight.

"Archie, you know the rules. No dessert tonight. Up to bed you go," Dad said, disappointed. Mom was busy comforting a distraught Sophia so I managed to avoid a lecture from her as I trudged up the stairs and into my room.

"Thanks a bunch, Lizzie, looks like you had enough cake so no tasty crickets for you this evening," I said, placing the lizard into a large glass tank beside my bed. *I've definitely had better Sundays,* I thought wryly, diving headfirst on top of my bed.

Sleep did not come easy.

As I lay in the near darkness – the dim light from the lizard tank always prevented total darkness, for which I was very grateful – I couldn't help but think back on my near-death encounter with the dog at Mr Schimmel's Sanctuary.

Another knot formed in my stomach as my thoughts turned to the dodgeball qualifier, two days away and getting closer by the minute.

I wasn't sure how long I had been lying there when I heard it.

Chirp.

A flutter of wings.

Chirp. Chirp. Chirp.

A dark shape moving across the room. Wait, no. Lots of dark shapes zooming in the dim light cast from Lizzie's tank.

Now a cacophony of chirping and rustling... diving towards me... claws and beaks ready to tear—

I woke in a cold sweat. The pounding of my heart vibrated in my ear. It had all been a dream.

I took a deep breath to calm himself. *It was only a dream,* I thought in an effort to slow my heart down.

Suddenly a small shadow darted across the ceiling and behind the wardrobe. I rubbed my eyes. I pinched my arm.

This time, I wasn't dreaming. Definitely not dreaming.

The bird was in my room.

I bolted for the bedroom door. I was halfway up the hall before I started to feel foolish. Why was I running from a little *bird*? A harmless, fluffy, yellow bird! What would Dad think if I ran into his room asking for help?

And if Sophia got wind of this... I didn't want to think of the fun she would have. She would never let me hear the end of it. That was for sure.

"Who's out there? Archie, is that you? What are you doing?"

"It's only me, Mom. Toilet break. Heading back to bed now. G'night."

I strode back to my room purposefully. Chest out. Fear tucked away.

I was being totally ridiculous. Huge hairy spiders and scaly gigantic snakes didn't scare me so why would I run from a tiny parakeet?

Even so, when I reached my bedroom door, I peeked cautiously into my room. Just because I didn't want to spook the bird or anything like that. Obviously.

I peered into all four corners of the room. No sign

of the bird. Maybe I had imagined the whole thing? Yes, I must have.

I bet the bird was still down where I left it. On the paint-chipped desk in the backyard zoo. Probably sleeping.

I chuckled at my own expense and made to get back into bed.

At least Sophia didn't see me—

"Ahhhhh!" I shrieked, falling on my backside as a dark shape flew out from behind the wardrobe.

The bird fluttered ungracefully around the ceiling. Travelling in circles, like a dog chasing its tail. Its leathery wings were beating wildly and erratically. Wait a minute— leathery wings? This was no bird!

The bat flitted towards the open window and exited out into the jet-black darkness.

I bolted the window closed, wiped sweat off my forehead and let out a sigh of relief.

"Don't look at me like that, Lizzie. My sugar levels must be low today!"

****

The smell of a grilled toasted cheese wafted up to my room from the downstairs kitchen. It tickled my nose, inviting me to wake up and start the day. It almost got me out of bed. Almost.

I felt like I hadn't slept at all. I rolled over and was immediately met by a wet, slobbering tongue on my face.

"Morning Buster," I mumbled, blinking away the sleep from my eyes. The great thing about Buster was that I didn't need an alarm clock to wake me up for school, I had Buster to do that for me.

"It's only 7:45 Buster, I still have another 15 minutes."

The week I had been dreading had finally begun. Tomorrow, there was a high probability that I would embarrass myself in front of the whole school. And to make matters worse, I would let the whole school down in the process if we didn't make the nationals. My tummy was in knots, maybe I'd skip the toasted cheese sambo this morning.

Bangs and crashes from downstairs brought me out of my gloomy thoughts. What was all the commotion?

"Archie!" shouted Mom. "Get down here this instant!"

"Uh oh Buster—this doesn't sound good."

Accompanied by Buster, I grabbed my glasses and lazily made my way downstairs. When I entered the kitchen, I saw Mom with her hands on her hips. She was still in her nurse overalls. Of all times of the day to frustrate her, after a night shift at work was the worse.

I wonder what I done now?

"Archie Jones! March out to that garage right now and help your Father. I don't know what's got into you lately but I'm fed up with your carelessness," she said, nodding her head in disbelief.

I could only scratch my head in confusion as I had no idea what this was all about.

Mom turned her back to me and began forcefully

throwing last night's dishes into the sink.

Taking the hint that it was time to go, I made my way out back to the garage under a marble grey sky. A cold wind blew. Goosebumps covered my arms.

Should have brought a jumper.

The best way to describe the scene that met me in the garage was to say it looked as if a herd of rhinos had stampeded through. The place was upside down. Containers were spilled across the dirt floor. One wire mesh shelf had toppled over, bringing with it multiple forms of animal medication and papers. Crickets were literally everywhere! Matilda the tarantula was halfway up the back wall. Arnold was nibbling on some loose papers. Trevor was halfway out of his glass tank, forked tongue testing the free air.

In the midst of the chaos, Dad was on his hands and knees, scurrying around with a plastic box, attempting to catch as many crickets as possible.

The only animal that seemed to have avoided the destruction was our newest inhabitant. The golden parakeet sat where I had left him the night before. Untouched and undisturbed.

I gave my glasses a good wipe with my pyjama top. "Dad, what happened?"

Breathing heavily, Dad lifted his head.

"Arch, do you want to explain this? Your mother is at the end of her tether. She's considering pulling the plug on our little garage zoo project."

"But Dad, I didn't do this. Honestly!" I pleaded.

"Maybe I have been a bit careless letting you look after all of these animals at your age. Perhaps your

Mom is right, and we should look to re-home these guys."

My eyes widened in disbelief. I felt my upper lip quiver.

"Dad... no. Please! You gotta believe me!"

I was desperate. The animals were my life. My only friends. I couldn't lose them.

"Look my boy, if it wasn't you, then who else? We both know your mom and sister won't set foot in here. They're creeped out by some of our hairier friends," he said as he pointed to the large spider, almost tasting freedom near a small opening of a window.

I glanced accusingly towards the bird cage and the golden bird within. It stared innocently back.

Chirp.

"Oh no you don't. You hardly think I'll entertain that idea, Arch. Now clean this mess up and we can put it behind us."

"I know, Dad, but—"

"No buts, Arch. You were the last one in here, *correct?*" Dad glanced at his wristwatch. "Gosh would you look at the time, I'm going to be late for work!"

He waddled towards the door, pulling on his khaki Gentry Park Zoo pullover. He looked back towards me.

"Can I trust you to have this place spick and span?"

"Yes Sir," I said quietly.

"That's my boy!" And he was gone.

I sighed and surveyed the wreckage in front of me. I had no choice but to clean the mess I didn't make. The thoughts of parting with my animal friends were too much to bear. I couldn't let that happen.

But then, who was responsible for this? Probably Sophia trying to land me in it again.

It took me just under a half hour to return the garage to its original state. All animals were returned to their cages, tanks or containers. Except for the crickets, I was certain the majority of these had escaped.

"Archie, are you still out there? You're going to be late for the bus," came Mom's voice from the backyard.

I took one last look at the bird who gawked at me innocently, before covering its cage with a blanket and sprinting upstairs, quickly donning my school uniform. This consisted of two attempts as I stupidly put my pants on back to front on the first try.

Taking the stairs two at a time, I darted out the front door—just in time to see the school bus pass. Sophia waved merrily at me from her window seat aboard the bus.

Sighing miserably for what wasn't the first time this morning, I began the two block walk to school. The marble sky darkened, heavy drops of rain began to fall.

Surely the day couldn't get any worse.

Well, it could. And it would.

Montgomery Elementary School is thankfully a relatively short walk from home. Be that as it may, the combination of a growling empty stomach that didn't have time for breakfast and the steady downpour of rain made it feel an awful lot longer.

To make matters worse, in my frantic haste to make the bus, I left the house without my companion, Lizzie. It was like leaving a body part behind. I couldn't remember the last time I went to school without my scaly friend.

With the help of a friendly lollipop lady, I crossed the road and entered the school grounds, which were flanked by large stone pillars. The school crest was embedded in each pillar.

Dripping wet, I entered the bustling school corridors. I brushed wet, matted hair from my forehead and strode towards the lockers.

I looked like a drowned rat!

It was hard not to notice the stares. Kids mockingly pointed at the trail of wetness I was leaving behind.

I really ought to find a hair dryer and stand under

it for a while.

Ignoring the onlookers, I turned a corner and edged my way past a boy and girl who seemed to be exchanging phone numbers.

I opened my locker and—

SMACK!

Blinding white lights dotted across my vision. Pain flowed like a tidal wave from the back of my head. Tenderly touching my throbbing skull, I turned around.

"Dr Dolittle! Is that how you dodge a ball? Movement like that won't help the team in the game tomorrow. Also, why do you look like you just got out of your annual bath?"

Dylan Harrison, otherwise known as 'Skid', was one of the meanest kids in school. He was built like a rhino from his bulky frame to his aggressive personality - always ready to charge. He wore his dark brown hair in a mullet style which had the effect of reminding me of rat's tails.

Skid has been torturing me ever since kindergarten. I'm not sure why, maybe I was an easy target? Or because I have flaming ginger hair? Or that I (usually) carry a lizard around in my pocket? Who knows! Bullies don't always give reasons!

He held a red dodgeball under one burly arm. A dodgeball that was currently imprinted on the back of my head. At his side were his motley crew of tormentors.

"What do you want, Dylan?" I said, wincing at the small bump that had emerged among my ginger curls.

"What do I want? From _you_? Nothing. Well, I want nothing right now."

I breathed a sigh of relief.

"But…if you cost us the game tomorrow," he bunched his thick fists menacingly, "you will have more to worry about than just my Dad flunking you. You got that, Dolittle?"

Did I mention Coach Harrison is Dylan's Dad? No? Well, he is.

Dylan's cronies all laughed on cue. I reckon they were just as terrified of him as I was. For that reason, I wouldn't have called them his friends exactly. More like minions who tolerated him out of fear.

"Message understood, Dylan," I said submissively.

"It's _Skid_, Dolittle!" He was just about to practice his best dodgeball throw again when the bell rang.

Phew.

He shoved me against the lockers and walked off with his fellow group of bullies in tow.

I collected my books and made my way to the temporary safety of Miss Jacobs' history class.

I slouched in my seat by the window. Sopping wet, exhausted from last night's broken sleep and head aching from the whack of a dodgeball.

"Archie, is everything alright?" said a kind voice. "Why are you rubbing your head like that?" Hannah Somers sat in the desk directly opposite me.

What I really liked about Hannah, other than how her dimples appeared when she smiled, was that she didn't join in on the laughter that time my shorts fell down at track practice. Or call me mean names like *Dr Dolittle*.

I began to explain what happened but stopped abruptly when I spotted Skid Harrison glaring menacingly at me from across the classroom.

"Erm, yeah. Everything's fine, Hannah. Just a bad night's sleep is all."

Hannah raised her eyebrows, shrugged her shoulders and returned her attention to Miss Jacobs' lesson.

I found myself gazing listlessly out of the window onto the school grounds as Miss Jacobs started to list prominent World War II battles on the whiteboard.

Directly in my line of view, an old chestnut tree stood proudly under a patch of now blue sky. An energetic grey squirrel scuttled playfully in and around the tree. Just visible behind the tree, a man in paint-flecked grey overalls observed the squirrel keenly. Notebook in hand, he scribbled away as the squirrel nibbled on its prized chestnut.

I knew this man not only as the new school caretaker, but as my friend. We had a lot in common. For one, the kids here at school also made fun of him for being different. Most importantly, we share the same enthusiasm when it comes to the animal kingdom. He once helped me nurse an injured sparrow back to health and ever since then we got on like zebras and ostriches.

"Archie Jones, are you paying attention?"

Snapping out of my daydream-like state, I returned my attention to Miss Jacobs' history lesson. I concentrated on the whiteboard and tried to follow the movement of the marker as she noted down the key dates of battles.

The classroom was stuffy, heat turned up unnecessarily high.

No matter how hard I tried, I could feel a weight on my eyelids, inevitably forcing them shut. I slapped my cheeks. I forced my eyelids open with pen caps but nothing was working. Like an elevator door, my eyes kept slamming shut.

In an effort to remain alert, I gazed back out of the window. Maybe the caretaker would be up to something fun. Like climbing the tree to study the bird nests or something crazy.

But he had since left and was probably off elsewhere either tending to the needs of the school or taking notes on the local wildlife.

I stared at the old chestnut tree. Several birds were perched in the branches. And that's when I spotted it.

At first, I was sure my eyes were deceiving me. Among the blackbirds and the white/grey sparrows was another colour. A very bright colour. Golden yellow.

The parakeet from Mr Schimmel's had followed me to school.

Chirp.

"Nooooooo!" I shouted, falling out of my seat.

The school bell rang at precisely the same time as my panicked yelp. Luckily for me, this prevented half of the class from hearing my high-pitched shriek and witnessing my ungraceful fall to the floor. The other half of the class, the one that regrettably included Hannah Somers, gazed at me with looks of curiosity, ridicule and some faces wore that look you get when you realise you have just stepped in something disgusting.

Red faced, I climbed to my feet and packed away my textbook. I pretended to be busy while the class emptied. I wasn't in the mood to talk to anyone.

"Everything OK, Mr Jones?"

"Yes Miss Jacobs, just tying my shoelace."

My shoes didn't even have laces.

Before I left, I peered towards the chestnut tree, seeking out the source of my panic. Seeking to prove that I wasn't going crazy. Blackbirds, sparrows and starlings perched on the large branches innocently. But there were no golden yellow feathers to be seen.

****

The school canteen rang with the noises of lunchtime. Kids laughed, shouted, argued and slapped each other high fives. Tables and benches were lined horizontally in three separate rows as kids filed down the aisles towards seats held by their friends, especially for them.

I plonked myself down on an empty bench and emptied the contents of my lunchbox onto the table. Mom had packed me a salad sandwich and a green apple. Great! Mom always said it was important to get the week off to a healthy start. I, on the other hand, would have preferred to be tucking into a nice crunchy chocolate bar.

My stomach tightened as I spotted Hannah Somers walking towards my bench. She brushed her chestnut hair off her shoulder, smiled widely and waved enthusiastically in my direction.

Maybe I could explain to her why I was behaving weird today. Or rather, weirder than normal.

Surprised and a little bit nervous, I raised my hand in greeting and was just about to say "*Hi*" when Hannah continued on past me, taking a seat with a group of her friends. The group of friends who she was clearly waving at.

I scratched my head in an obvious effort to cover up my foolishness.

Unsuccessfully.

"Who are you waving at, Archie?" Sophia had just walked into the canteen with her cackling entourage.

"Erm…" I struggled to think of an excuse that wouldn't make me seem so pathetic in front of

Sophia and her groupies.

"H-he was w-waving at m-me."

The nervous caretaker, Bob Hope, came up behind the girls, startling them at the same time. He lowered himself onto the bench opposite me.

Sophia bit her lower lip, frowning at the interrupter who had unknowingly ruined her fun. She scrunched up her face, as if she was about to say something, then seemed to decide against it. After all, as caretaker, Bob was a member of the school faculty and could easily report any misbehaviour to the school principal. Sophia might be a walking nightmare but she wasn't stupid.

Sophia and the gang took one last look at the caretaker before swaggering off in the opposite direction, rolling their eyes in unison.

"Hi Bob."

"Hi Archie. It's not v-very nice when your sister t-treats you like that. She should be k-kind to her big b-brother," Bob said, smiling.

Bob has been nothing but nice to me since he joined the school a couple of weeks back. Like me, he always seems to be on his own. I don't think I've ever seen him having lunch with the other teachers or even talking to another adult.

It doesn't help his case that Montgomery Elementary is full of mean kids who are only happy to constantly remind Bob of his speech issues. That, combined with his nervousness, makes him an easy target for bullies, even though he is a grown adult.

"Awh, I just ignore her, Bob. No point in getting

into a fight with an eleven-year-old girl, right?" I said wryly.

Bob brushed a strand of greasy black hair off his pale face. His dark eyes darted from side to side. I'm not sure why but he could never make eye contact.

Poor guy.

"Suppose not. How's L-Lizzie?"

I reached into my pocket before remembering sadly that I had left my scaly friend at home. It was probably for the best. The last time I had decided to let Lizzie out to stretch her legs, the lunchroom erupted in chaos. This wasn't the only animal-related mayhem involving me either. This one time, I brought Matilda in for show and tell and let's just say I got to show everyone the tarantula but I never got to the tell part. Kids jumped on desks, Rachel Myers fainted and Mark Hamilton literally got up from his desk and ran out of the class. It didn't do much to enhance my popular reputation. Even the kind Hannah Somers moved her desk a couple of yards away back from mine that day.

"Lizzie's doing great, although she got me in a lot of trouble last night. Turns out she is fond of birthday cake!" I said with a smirk.

Bob chuckled, rocking back and forth on the bench. He cast nervy glances over his shoulder, as if expecting someone to sneak up behind him.

Bob took out his journal from a back pocket and began to scribble intensely. When he wasn't chatting with me, he was forever buried in his journal. Sometimes, like right now, he would lose himself in the journal and I'd have to remind him I was still here.

Before I got the chance to, he spoke up: "Something on your mind, A-Archie?" Bob kept his eyes downcast, focussed on whatever sketch he was working on. I could make out the tail of a squirrel maybe.

Although we had only known each other for less than two whole months, we had struck up a close friendship and Bob could tell when I was in a foul mood or had something on my mind that was bugging me.

"I can't say I'm exactly looking forward to the dodgeball game tomorrow. And it's been a bit crazy at home lately," I sniffed.

"I think you will do great, Archie. I'll be c-cheering you on, I p-promise," Bob said reassuringly.

****

The sun was setting behind our house when the school bus pulled into the street, casting long dark shadows across the lawn. A bitter breeze blew into my face as I stepped off the bus, stinging my face and hands. It was going to be a cold night.

Sophia rushed past me, hollering goodbye to her bus friends, making sure she bumped me on the shoulder as she ran through the front door and climbed the stairs, two steps at a time.

Mom was in the hall as I shut the front door against the outside chill.

"Hi Arch, how was your day?" she said as she mopped the floor, again in her nurse overalls. It felt like she had them on all day every day.

"Fine Mom. Just your usual Monday—"

I was interrupted as Sophia came hurtling past me, knocking the school bag off my shoulder in the process.

"Soph, walk please, you will slip and break your neck! Can't you see the floor is wet?"

"Sorry Mom," she shouted from the kitchen.

I trudged up to my room, throwing my bag on the floor among a pile of clothes and encyclopedias.

"Lizzie, sorry I left you alone today. Anything exciting happen while I was gone?" I said as I walked over to the glass tank.

I looked into the tank.

But Lizzie was nowhere to be seen.

I checked all corners of the tank, under the plants, in the water basin—but the spotted lizard had disappeared.

Lifting a rock in the centre of the tank where Lizzie sometimes hid in to shed her skin, I jumped back suddenly as if stung.

Lizzie wasn't under the rock. No, but something else was.

I found a lonely feather under the rock.

A golden yellow feather.

I was momentarily frozen. I didn't know what to think or how to feel. Several dark thoughts and impossible questions spiralled around inside my head.

What was a yellow feather doing in Lizzie's tank? How did it get there? Did it have something to do with the strange bird we took home from Mr Schimmel's sanctuary?

Before I went into a total panic, I decided to check my room thoroughly to make sure Lizzie hadn't simply escaped the tank—which had happened on a number of occasions previously. Too many occasions if truth be told.

I took a few lungfuls of air to calm my breathing. Then I searched every nook and cranny – behind the wardrobe, sifting through the messy pile of clothes on the floor, coughing among the dust underneath my bed. I even checked inside my sneakers (although I'm sure the odour would scary Lizzie off if anything).

No sign of my scaly friend.

Wait, maybe Lizzie was downstairs somewhere? Yes, that was a possibility! She loved to turn up in random places around the house and scare the life out of Mom and Sophia.

But then, how to explain the yellow feather in the lizard tank?

I knew what needed to be done. Although, I didn't want to admit it.

I had to be brave for once. Lizzie is my best pal. And right now, she could be in danger.

No alternative other than to go out to the backyard zoo and face the owner of the yellow feather – the creepy bird that I was beginning to think was connected to the strange things that had been happening around me lately.

I had to be sure Lizzie wasn't there. Or if she was, rescue her before it's too late.

I strode forwards towards the door and backwards away from the door, trying to work up the courage to face what was waiting for me downstairs. Muttering words of comfort to myself, I dropped to the floor and reached under the bed. My hand found an old cracked badminton racket – the only weapon I had at my disposal.

It would have to do.

****

I entered the garage in the same manner as I usually enter my double math lesson on a Friday morning; a feeling of dread in the pit of my stomach and on tip toes as I'm normally late, trying to creep into my seat before the teacher notices.

The first thing I noticed was the heavy silence. An eerie stillness hung over the garage. It reminded me of that awkward silence you get in funeral parlours. Those places were always packed with people yet uncomfortably silent.

Outside, the sky had darkened to a dull grey, casting the garage into shadows.

I could hear a soft pattering on the roof, as the rain started to gently beat down.

Glancing towards the back of the room, on the paint-chipped desk, perched the golden yellow parakeet in its beautiful antique cage. A picture of innocence and elegance.

An old furry blanket lay discarded on the floor, a couple of yards from the cage.

Wait a minute. Didn't I cover the cage with that blanket before I left this morning?

I was pretty certain that I did? But then again, I was rushing to catch the school bus.

I could see the bird clearly from where I stood, despite the sparse light. It was bathed in a halo-like glow from the fish tank to its rear. It looked so confident, so self-assured. Let's see how smug it is after it says hello to my little friend – I'm referring to my badminton racket by the way.

Surely I was being silly, ludicrous even, but I felt like the bird was sizing me up! Challenging me to a stare down. Seeing if I would falter or crumble in its presence. Its beady eyes locked on mine, unmoving.

Be brave, Archie, I told myself, racking my brain for any bits of information that could help me. My fuzzy brain recalled a *birds of prey* documentary I recently watched. The show focussed on eagles, the apex predator of the skies (which means they're top of the food chain) and their hunting habits. Images crossed my mind of hooked beaks ripping flesh from their prey and powerful talons sinking into helpless victims.

But I wasn't dealing with an apex predator here, I was dealing with a parakeet – a bird that can be taught vocabulary like a parrot and on occasion is known to regurgitate food for humans they consider as family members. Yuck!

I'm pretty sure an eagle wouldn't even waste their time hunting something this small.

Feeling bolder, I took one step towards the cage.

Then another.

I stared at the bird.

It stared back at me.

Another step.

Now I was next to the cage. I raised the badminton racket high. My arm shook, my voice quivered as I said: "W-what have done with Lizzie?"

The golden bird stared back. The rain started to drum loudly against the roof.

"Tell me what you done with her!" I said more forcefully. "We never should have taken you home, you aren't normal and you don't belong here."

A bead of sweat broke out on my forehead as the golden parakeet stared back, deadpan.

I thought of how ludicrous this situation was. Here I was, a twelve-year-old boy, using a badminton racket as a weapon, having a conversation with a little bird and accusing it of such crimes.

As I started to come to my senses, I lowered the

racket slowly.

And then, the bird cocked its head awkwardly to the side and opened its beak wide.

"*Lizzie was a tasty treat. You will never see her again, Archie,*" it rasped.

My jaw dropped. My insides seized. The badminton racket clattered to the floor. A scream got caught in the back of my throat.

I took a number of backward steps away from the cage, trying to comprehend the reality that I had a killer bird for a pet.

A killer bird who had kidnapped and more than likely ate my best friend, Lizzie.

Suddenly, I heard a snigger. It was coming from behind the bird cage and under the table.

I knew who that snigger belonged to.

Sophia burst out from her hiding place, covering her mouth with her hands in disbelief that her prank had worked.

"Gotcha, Archie! I can-not *believe* you actually thought my bird was having a conversation with you!" she sneered, dropping the raspy voice she had chosen for her trick. "How old are you again? Only *you* would fall for a prank like that! Ha ha, you should have seen your face!"

For about five seconds, I stood rooted to the spot, momentarily frozen in place. Then, my fear began to subside, to be replaced with a new emotion. An emotion that can be likened to how a bull feels when it spots a showy matador whipping their cape (bulls are colour blind, so it's not the red muleta that enrages them) around, goading them solely for the entertainment of bloodthirsty spectators.

If I owned a pair of sharp horns, I know exactly where I would be directing them right now. That would wipe the smirk off Sophia's face for sure!

"I knew it was you, Sophia – nice try. I was just playing along to see how long you could keep the joke going," I lied.

Gosh, how could I have been so stupid? I actually thought for a second I was speaking with a killer bird. Woah. That's a new low – even for me.

"Now, give me Lizzie back," I demanded shrilly. My voice came off squeaky, probably an aftereffect of the fright I just pretended I didn't get.

She took the trembling lizard out of her pocket. "Just admit that I got you good, Archie, and you can have Lizzie back," she said with a smug smile.

I glared at my sister, my temper rising by the second. If looks could kill...

"Hand her over now – she doesn't like you! If you knew anything about her you would know she is uncomfortable with the *stupid* way you're holding her!" I barked.

Lizzie was frantically trying to escape. In fact, it was amazing that Sophia was able to keep a hold on the struggling lizard. Lizzie didn't take kindly to strangers and was only really comfortable when I held her.

In an effort to keep her under control, Sophia squeezed, rather too tightly and I spotted Lizzie's eyes bulge slightly. A fuse was about to blow inside me. I took a menacing step towards Sophia, fists clenched.

Spotting my intentions, Sophia wound back her arm and fired Lizzie through the air.

"Here... CATCH," she shouted.

I dove through the air.

Time seemed to slow down as I watched the spotted lizard descend to the floor. Like one of those slow-motion movie scenes.

With my arms outstretched to their physical limits, I landed heavily on my chest, knocking the breath out of my lungs at the same time. Just in time as Lizzie landed comfortably in my palms. It was a catch that any pro baseball player would be proud of.

I tried to breathe a sigh of relief but I was struggling to get the air back into my lungs.

"Phew – that was a close one, Lizzie," I gasped to the now calm Lizzie, unaware of how close she had come to splatting on the floor.

"Smile for the camera, Archie." Sophia walked towards where I lay on the dirt floor, her new iPhone held out in front of her.

"This video might make me famous you know. I could be the next YouTube sensation! I've actually been meaning to start a new vlogging channel," she said, fingers tapping against her lips as if in contemplation. "The minute I post this up, it will go viral at school and then probably the world! I'll have a million subscribers in no time!"

I looked up at her in stunned disbelief. Not only had Sophia made a complete fool out of me, she had been recording the whole thing! Clearly, she hid the phone somewhere in the garage and hit record before I came in.

She must have caught everything on video! Me cautiously creeping into the garage with the racket held high – woah I must have looked ridiculous. Next, speaking and actually threatening a tiny yellow bird – super embarrassing. And worse of all, my scaredy-cat reaction when I heard the bird – or rather Sophia – speak to me.

I couldn't show my face in school if this got uploaded to the internet. I mean, it's not that I was worried about becoming any less popular, but there were certain people in school I would prefer didn't see footage of me making an ape of myself. Certain dimple-faced people, with chestnut hair that smelled of flowers...

"Delete that video NOW!" I shouted.

"No... I don't think I'll do that. I think I'll send it to Hannah Somers and see what she has to say—"

That was it. The straw that broke the camel's back as the old saying goes.

Leaping like a frog, I sprung to my feet and charged at Sophia, reaching for the phone. Grabbing a hold of each other, we tussled and tumbled. I pinched her arm. She pulled my hair. There was a lot of shouting, scratching and name calling.

Meanwhile, the yellow parakeet looked on indifferently, as if it was bored by our scuffle.

I used my superior twelve-year-old weight to push Sophia backwards. With a loud crash, we collided with one of the wire mesh shelves, upending containers, animal food, glass tanks and old tools.

"Noooooo," Sophia wailed. "Look what you did, you *jerk*!"

Her brand-new iPhone lay face-up on the ground, multiple cracks indented on the screen.

"You are going to be in sooo much trouble when I tell Mom—"

But I wasn't paying attention to Sophia or to the broken phone. I was staring at something else.

An occupant had escaped from one of the glass tanks that hit the floor a moment ago. A slithery occupant. Trevor, the red and black coral snake, was slithering up the leg of the paint-chipped table, making his way towards the antique bird cage.

Sophia had also forgotten her precious broken phone and was now gazing terrified at the unfolding scene.

The parakeet eyed the oncoming predator as it slithered slowly into the birdcage, forked tongue testing the air, trying to locate the ideal place to strike for the kill.

The bird cocked its head to the side, oblivious to the imminent danger it was in.

Faster than a viper's strike, Trevor attacked, intent on making the golden bird its next meal.

Sophia covered one eye, trying to but unable to look away. I could only stare, open-mouthed.

In the blinking of an eye, the hunter became the prey. The parakeet opened its beak unnaturally wide, catching the oncoming snake by the head and slurping the rest of its body down like a string of spaghetti.

And just like that, Trevor was gone.

"Archie... d-did my bird just eat that snake?" Sophia asked, dumbfounded.

We looked at each other, confused and scared. The parakeet belched loudly after its meal.

Then it looked straight at me.

Chirp.

"That did not just happen... TELL ME that did not happen!"

"Sophia, it happened! We both saw it with our own eyes," I said to my terror-stricken sister. She was sitting on my bedroom floor, head cradled between her arms, sobbing softly.

"I knew something wasn't right about that animal sanctuary. In fact, I doubt it's even a real sanctuary at all! More like some strange animal prison where all of the animals are crazy. And let's not forget Mr Schimmel. He's easily the creepiest person I've ever met! I bet he's the one behind this," I said assuredly.

We didn't linger about the backyard zoo after the bird eating the snake incident. After a very brief argument over whose job it was to cover the birdcage with the blanket – an argument I lost due to a game of rock, paper, scissors – we swiftly exited the garage. We were stunned. Terrified. How could a little yellow parakeet consume a reptile that was at least five times its length? I know that snakes are able to consume prey three times larger than the width of their heads, but I'm pretty sure parakeets don't possess that ability!

Dinner that evening was a fairly subdued event. Mom sensed something was up with us, but she put it down to Dad being away on his work trip and her new falafel recipe that was untouched on our plates. With all that had been going on, I forgot Dad was leaving for his work trip today. *Trevor was his favourite pet,* I thought sadly.

Head down, I toyed with my food, pushing it from one side of the plate to the other. I couldn't get the image out of my head of poor Trevor disappearing down the bird's beak. I would probably need a few years of counselling for that to be possible.

We both agreed not to mention this to Mom until we figured out what was going on. She probably wouldn't have believed us anyway. I mean, I wouldn't have believed the story unless I had witnessed it with my own two eyes. It's likely that she would assume we carelessly let Trevor escape and then she would call Dad who would probably come straight home from his trip, leaving us in a world of trouble. After all, she was still convinced it was my fault all of the animals had escaped from their respective homes this morning!

After Mom had finally accepted that the falafels would remain uneaten, she excused us from the table. We darted upstairs to my room, where we were now discussing the predicament we found ourselves in.

"But how can a little yellow bird be evil? It just doesn't make sense! You're the animal expert, Arch, have you and Dad ever seen anything like this before?" Sophia asked, raising her head from between her legs.

"Well, Dad once told me about a species of eagle that eat snakes but we're talking about a pet parakeet here!" I scratched my head and pushed my glasses further up on my nose. "No, something is not normal with this bird. Did you see how wide its beak opened? And those black eyes, it's almost as if the bird is eyeing you up as its next meal! It gives me the creeps!"

"We have got to tell Dad—he will know what to do," she said pleadingly.

I tipped a number of live crickets into Lizzie's tank as my brow furrowed in concentration. She snatched the first one that ventured too near. Unlike Sophia and I, Lizzie's appetite remained unaffected by the evening's events.

"No," I said after a number of seconds of deliberation. "Think about how it would sound. 'Hi Dad, eh... so you know Trevor the snake? Yep, well he's been eaten. By what? Oh, you know that yellow harmless bird we got on Sunday? Yes, that's right, the bird swallowed the snake'. There is no way he'll believe us. And even if he did, he can't help us all the way from San Francisco."

Sophia stood up.

"So, what do we do then? Pretend nothing happened and just go on with our lives? I'm not living in the same house as a killer bird, Archie... out of the question!" she shouted.

"Shh! Keep your voice down. I just need some time to figure this out. I know someone who may be able to help us." I pushed my glasses further up on my long nose.

"Who? The police?"

"No, you birdbrain! Sorry – bad choice of words. The only other person I can think of who can help us is Bob—"

"Archie no way, the caretaker's a freak! Just because he is nice to you doesn't mean he can help us."

"You don't understand, he knows more about animals than I do... maybe even more than Dad. Have you seen that notebook he carries around with him? It's like his own wildlife encyclopedia. I'm sure he will be able to help us," I said confidently.

"Fine, then call him."

The noise of the chirping crickets came to a halt as Lizzie gobbled the last one. Sophia's face twisted in a grimace. She wasn't cut out for the realities of the animal world like me.

"Don't have his number. But I have a better idea. I can bring the bird to school tomorrow and leave it with him. That way, it can't cause anymore mischief around the house which means I won't get in more trouble and Mom won't ground me for the whole summer!"

"I hope you're right, Arch, if he can't help us get rid of the killer bird then I'm sorry but I'm telling Mom," she said matter of factly on her way out of the room. "Oh, and Archie."

I looked up.

"You owe me a new iPhone."

****

It was another night of restless sleep for me. I

twisted and turned so many times, I made myself dizzy. My mind was as active as a beehive.

Would the caretaker know what to do with a murderous parakeet? Was I putting my family in danger by not telling Mom and Dad what happened? What if the bird escaped and got into my room tonight?

When I finally drifted off to sleep, I dreamt I was in a small cage, being poked with a sharp stick by none other than Mr Schimmel who laughed cruelly, his eyes burning an ember red.

Montgomery Elementary School was alive with excitement. It was typically a noisy school; you were always going to get that when you had a mix of grades one through eight piled into one building. Today, however, was exceptionally boisterous for it was an opportunity for the school to make it to the national finals in the sport the school was best known for—dodgeball.

The trophy cabinet beside the school principal's office contained many relics of the successes achieved by previous middle grade teams from the school. Only, there had not been an addition to the trophy cabinet for almost three years now and the pressure was on.

Coach Harrison was in a crazy mood the past number of weeks. Between organising extra training sessions for the team, sticking game day posters all over the school – much to Principal Heeney's annoyance – and even carrying a dodgeball under his arm at all times, he was a man best avoided. He wanted to win so badly.

Today, he was behaving like a man possessed. He would sneak up behind players on the team and shout

'DODGE', and if they didn't move fast enough they would receive a cold hard ball to the back of the head.

I, believe it or not, had forgotten all about the big game. I had been so preoccupied with the evil bird and my plan to get rid of it that the game slipped my mind completely.

It was only when I walked through the school entrance and spotted the red school banners streaming up and down the corridor, that I realised what day it was. Monty the school mascot – a proud goat – glared down at me, with an expression that said, 'Do not screw up today, Archie'. I always thought it was a dumb mascot. I mean, of all animals to choose from, our school picked a goat?

Sophia had also left me to fend for myself with *her* bird and birdcage.

"No way will I be seen carrying that thing around. Sorry Arch, I have a reputation to protect. I'll catch-up with you later." And she had disappeared into the back of the school bus.

Nothing appeared to have changed with her anyway!

So, I had to lug the awkward antique cage onto the bus – amid the stares and sneers of the other kids – carry it into the school and then look for Bob the caretaker.

As I hurriedly rounded the corner by my locker, again ignoring the spectators who whispered and pointed at the odd shape under the blanket, I smacked straight into none other than Skid Harrison. My glasses flew off my nose as I fell onto my backside.

The birdcage rattled onto the floor, clanging loudly in the corridor, drawing even more stares.

"Dolittle!" Skid shouted as he turned around and saw me sprawled on the corridor.

I made to grab for my glasses but was too slow as Skid stuck out a foot and dragged them out of my reach. Skid's usual cronies sniggered.

"Well well well, what do we have here?" he said, spotting the birdcage.

"Nothing, Dylan, its none of your business anyway," I said crossly, crawling in front of the birdcage protectively.

"I think I'll make it my business—"

"D-Dylan Harrison, you leave him alone unless you want me to tell your Daddy about what you and your friends were d-doing to Principal Heeney's car last week," said Bob the caretaker in the nick of time. I was starting to lose count of the amount of times Bob had saved me from a pummelling.

Skid glared at the caretaker. He might not have been the sharpest tool in the shed but he wasn't stupid enough to mess with a member of the school faculty.

"I'll be seeing you later, Dolittle. And remember, you will have more to worry about than failing P.E. if you mess up," he said, banging his knuckles together menacingly.

Bob helped me to my feet.

"I'm fine, Bob, honestly. Thanks."

"You shouldn't let him p-push you around, Archie. Bu-bu-bullies need to be taught a lesson."

"Listen, Bob, I need some help. You see this bird here." I lifted the blanket slightly, revealing the golden bird beneath. Bob's dark eyes lit up. "Well, it's been acting very strange at home. Weird things have been happening around the house. I was hoping you could... well... observe it for a day or something? I'd ask my Dad but he's away on a work trip."

Bob took out his notebook and began to scribble, his tongue sticking out in concentration. He ignored me for the best part of two minutes before closing the notebook and saying: "Sure Archie, anything for a f-friend. Hakuna m-m-matata."

With that, the caretaker picked up the birdcage and headed off in the opposite direction without even a goodbye. I had expected him to have some questions but I was too relieved to care. I could hear Bob humming a dainty tune, as if he was singing a lullaby to a baby. He really did love animals.

The school bell rang, signalling the start of class. Kids ran in all directions.

My day can only get better from here, I thought to myself.

I was wrong.

The rules of dodgeball are quite straightforward. DO NOT GET HIT BY THE BALL. That was the easiest one to remember—and the most important.

Truth be told, I wasn't overly familiar with the rules of the sport. I should have known them quite well actually – it was a regular activity on the school P.E. rota – but I was prone to mysteriously falling ill every Thursday afternoon... around 13:45pm... just before P.E. would start.

The big game was taking place during lunchtime, so I had to use my double geography lesson to brush up on the remaining rules of dodgeball. Phone concealed between my textbook, I learned that each team starts with four players on the court. There are four balls in play at all times; each team starts with one each and the other two are up for grabs on the center line at the beginning of each game.

A player exits the game if they get hit by the ball below the shoulders; if the opposing team catches a ball thrown by that player or if they cross the centre line during the game.

Simple!

However, the greatest rule in the history of

dodgeball – in my opinion, of course – was that substitutions can only be made in the event of an injury to another player.

Yesssss, I thought. *How many injuries are possible in a ten-minute game?*

The discovery of this beautiful rule helped ease my nerves. The four other players on the team were real tough kids. Marty Bradshaw, Cian Sampson and Holly Parker were some of the meanest kids in the seventh grade. They were all big, scary and possibly quite wealthy from all of the lunch money they had stolen. Of course, Skid Harrison, their self-appointed leader, was the toughest of them all. The alpha bully. The king of the jungle in bully terms.

There was *no way* they could get injured. I once saw Holly Parker take a frisbee to the head and she didn't even flinch! My plan was to just sit on the sidelines and cheer on the bully squad.

Coach Harrison would then pass me in P.E. and I wouldn't have to spend the summer locked in my room! And more importantly, Mom wouldn't make us get rid of the backyard zoo.

This day was turning out to be quite OK after all.

****

The basketball-turned-dodgeball court was packed to the rafters. It looked as if the whole school had come to support the team. The opposition team from MacMillan Elementary School had also brought along a strong number of supporters who were making their presence known. They occupied the left-hand side of the court. A noisy sea of blue and white, a buffalo emblazoned on their jumpers, tees and caps. A much more impressive mascot than our goat!

The Montgomery students and teachers, clad in the red school colours, sat in the bleachers on the right-hand side of the court. Both sides of the hall cheered and sang for their team.

"We are the Montgomery Goats,
And we can't be beat
Because we got the power,
to knock you off your feet!"

The rivalry was intense! MacMillan Elementary was, after all, only a couple of blocks away from Montgomery.

"Strong, blue and a little white,
We're the Buffalos,
And we'll fight, fight, fight!"

Coach Harrison was giving a lively pep talk to the team who were in a huddle formation at the side of the court. I stood awkwardly behind the huddle, content not to be part of the camaraderie. I didn't fancy getting spittle on my face from the red-faced coach anyway.

Above the buzz of the court, I made out a few choice words from the P.E. coach: '*destroy*', '*dodge*', '*punish*', '*no mercy*', '*dodge*'.

Gazing into the crowd, I spotted Hannah Somers, smiling and running her hands through her hair.

My stomach churned with nerves. You know that feeling when you think a kaleidoscope of butterflies are fluttering in your stomach?

I really didn't want to make a fool of myself in front of Hannah.

A man in black and white stripes took to the court, counted the players on both sides and blew his whistle shrilly. The crowd roared.

It was dodgeball time!

I winced as one of the MacMillan players took a heavy blow to the mid-riff from Skid Harrison. Woah! The game had only started and they were one player down thanks to my tormentor. Skid's fist pumped the air as he shouted a battle cry.

Red balls whirled across the court as both teams threw at their targets. It was an intense match. The three remaining players from MacMillan were giving a good account of themselves. They dodged, ducked, dipped and dived much to the delight of their travelling support.

A raucous cheer went up from the blue side when a dodgeball thrown by Marty Bradshaw was caught comfortably, ending his game.

After a frantic five minutes, one more player from each team exited the game in comical fashion. Cian Sampson ran towards a loose ball in the centre of the court. He put his hands on it as it rolled onto the centre line, just as an opposing player wrapped their hands on it too. Both players grappled and managed to fall into the opposing team's zone.

I laughed along with the crowd. This was turning out to be quite enjoyable. Well, from the sidelines anyway.

Holly Parker advanced toward the centre line, winding up and letting loose a thunderbolt of a throw that stung the legs of a short stocky boy in blue. MacMillan were down to just one player! Montgomery were on the verge of going to the nationals!

But something was wrong with Holly. She was sitting on the court clasping her ankle in obvious pain.

Oh no no no. Please get up, Holly, PLEASE.

Coach Harrison looked at me, acknowledging my presence for the first time.

"Jones! You're in the game."

And with that, I was standing in the middle of the court beside a bemused looking Skid Harrison. I felt so small standing there, and not just because the team jersey and shorts were two sizes too big for me. The school gym somehow felt bigger with all of those eyes on me. Cheering me on but ready to turn on me in a moment's notice.

Skid Harrison tossed me a ball.

"Aim for the legs, Dolittle. And don't miss, ya little twerp!"

I was terrified. I wanted to drop the ball and run out of the hall. But, the other team did only have one player left. And I had Skid on my side! For once.

I focussed with all my might on my fuzzy target. Being short-sighted, it would have been much easier to see my opponent if Skid had given me back my glasses from earlier.

The crowd roared in anticipation.

I took aim at the blue blur outline of a boy across the hall and was about to let loose when I heard it.

Chirp.

I slipped and lost my balance mid-throw, head spinning wildly looking for the source of the dreaded chirping that I knew only too well. As I plunged to the wooden floor, the dodgeball left my hand. I heard a hard *thud*. A sure sound of a direct hit.

A groan rose up from the crowd.

Did I win the game for Montgomery?

I lifted my head and recoiled in fear. Skid was striding towards me with a bloody nose. A nose that was bloody because of me.

"Uh oh," was all I could say as I waited for the inevitable pounding from Skid who was ignoring the fact that the game was still in play!

More noise erupted from the packed crowd. Not cheers this time but shouts and cries... of panic. I looked up. Dogs, goats, cats and even rabbits were running wildly all over the school hall.

Where did they come from? Why did it look like they were attacking the other kids?

"Say goodnight, Dolittle."

Blurry white stars exploded in front of me as Skid smashed a dodgeball against my head.

I passed out among the chaos.

A blinding white light stung my eyes.

"Wh-where am I? Did I die?"

"No Mr Jones, you're very much alive. You're in Nurse Jenkins office, having taken a bad blow to the head during that barbaric game. I'll be having words with Coach Harrison to have it banned once and for all, let me tell you."

As my vision came back into focus, I noticed I was lying on a makeshift bed that was used for students who needed medical care. Nurse Jenkins had just put away the torch she was shining directly at me, tut-tutting all the while. She was a tall, stern woman with jet black short cropped hair. She was dressed just like my mom.

"What happened? Did we win? Did you see a yellow bird? Where did all those animals come from?"

"Shush! A yellow what? Never mind that, Mr Jones. You need to rest up before your mother arrives to take you home—"

I sat upright in the bed and instantly felt dizzy. My head throbbed. A lump the size of a tennis ball was sprouting out the side of my head. Nurse Jenkins eased me back onto the trolley bed.

"As I was saying, Mr Jones, I want you to rest up for the evening. That means slow movements and no excitement. Plenty of rest. Got it?"

"Yes, Nurse Jenkins."

A short while later a rap on the door announced the arrival of my very concerned mom. She spoke briefly with Nurse Jenkins, thanking her before putting an arm tenderly around my shoulders and leading me out of the school. The red SUV was parked by the curb.

We passed many kids on the way out of school and from the way they looked at me, I knew Montgomery were not going to the nationals this year. I also knew that was partly down to me.

"What are we waiting for, Mom, can't we just go home?" I pressed a cold pack on my throbbing head, wincing at the icy burn against my skin.

"We're waiting on your sister, Arch. Didn't you hear? They had to close the school for the day. I got a call from the secretary to come collect you both. They said classes would resume as normal tomorrow morning."

"But why are they closing today?" I asked, confused. I felt the onset of a headache.

"I didn't have time to ask, I had to get Majella to cover my shift and I left straight away when I heard you were hurt. Ask your sister, here she is now."

Sophia skipped up to the car and hopped in the back seat beside me. She looked super happy about something.

"Now *here* is the most popular kid in school... NOT! Arch, I can't believe you managed to hit not only your own teammate but Skid Harrison! I actually think he might have killed you if he wasn't distracted by that goat that was nibbling on his jersey."

"What goat? What happened, Sophia? Where did all those animals come from?"

"Beats me. I was watching the game with the girls, waiting for you to embarrass yourself and next thing I knew, cats, mice, goats and all other kinds of animals were running across the gym. They must have got in the emergency exit? Anyway, they ran all over the school and thrashed a bunch of classrooms. Some kid got hurt pretty bad by an angry black ram. It was crazy! That's why they let us leave this early," Sophia explained.

My head was starting to hurt even more. What was going on? I definitely heard that familiar chirping sound. It was so clear! And then animals just attack the school? What was this, the animal apocalypse?

"Dylan is going to kill me tomorrow," I groaned.

"He sure is, but that's something to worry about tomorrow. Did you get rid of the bird? Did the *dorky* caretaker take her?" Sophia kept her voice low. Mom was on her headset in the middle of a work conversation. We couldn't tell her the bird was no longer at home.

"He sure did, no thanks to you! Maybe you should be nicer to Bob, he didn't have to take the ball of fluff that *you* brought into the house!"

"Whatever. I'm just glad it's gone. Last night was way creepy."

We sat in silence for the remainder of the short

journey home.

The SUV pulled into the asphalt driveway as the red afternoon sun was making its descent beyond our house, casting long shadows across the red bricks.

"Mom, I'm fine... honestly!"

She was fussing over me like a mother goose frets over her goslings. Sometimes I think she forgets that I'm almost thirteen years old, not five! But rather than argue, I let her ease me out of the car.

"Now as Nurse Jenkins said, I want you to take it easy—"

A shrill scream caused Mom to dig her fingers painfully into my shoulder. The noise appeared to have come from the house. Sophia had already made her way into the house. It was her scream. I was sure of it.

Mom forgot about my injury and ran towards the house, shouting: "Sophia what's wrong?"

Probably seen a spider, I thought, gradually making my way to the living room.

It wasn't a spider. I could have dealt with a spider.

No, it was something worse.

Something that I was completely unprepared for.

Mom looked confused as she stared from Sophia, hands cupping her mouth, to me, standing rigidly like a rock, mouth open in shock.

For in the middle of the living room was an antique birdcage.

And in the birdcage, perched the golden yellow parakeet.

"How many times do I have to tell you, Archie – no animals are allowed in this house... other than Buster!" Mom shouted angrily.

I couldn't move. I was speechless. Even Sophia was speechless, which doesn't happen very often, let me tell you. All we could do was look at each other, open mouthed and dumbstruck.

My mind stopped working. Like the batteries had run out.

How did the bird get back here? Did it hurt poor Bob? What did it want?

"Please get the bird out of my sight. I have to go into work and cover a shift. You're on your own tonight. Mrs Parkinson is going to check in on you. There is some leftover dinner in the fridge so help yourselves."

"Mom... I've decided I don't want the bird anymore. It might be best if we return it back where we got it from? I think it would be happier there," Sophia suggested.

I for one, was out of ideas as to what to do with the bird. My plan had failed. For once, Sophia was actually speaking some sense.

"Return it?" Mom gazed at the caged bird. A look of pity crossed her face. "You can't return a rescued pet you took home from a sanctuary Soph, that's not how it works, unfortunately. What will your Dad say when he gets home from his work trip and the parakeet is gone? You know how he feels about animals. Now, please take the cage out back. I don't want to see it in the house again."

"But Mom... the bird... well... it's evil," I said meekly. I felt silly saying it but I was literally out of ideas and telling the truth seemed like the only option left, even if it made me sound bonkers. Besides, parents always knew what to do in times of trouble.

That's their job!

Mom squinted at me concernedly and rested her hand on my forehead.

"You must have taken quite a whack to the head to be coming out with something as crazy as that. I want you to go straight up to your room with that cold press and take it easy for the evening, just like Nurse Jenkins instructed. I'll see you both in the morning."

As expected, it didn't work. Mom thought I was suffering from some sort of dodgeball-induced head trauma!

She grabbed her keys, quickly donned her coat and left the house promptly without another word.

I stared at Sophia helplessly. The reality sunk in that no-one would believe me. Who in their right mind would? Parakeets were harmless fluffy house pets. Not evil genius's hell-bent on destruction.

We were on our own and we knew it. And to make matters worse, we were home alone with a seven inch, evil, snake-eating parakeet.

*****

I lay on my bed, elbow propped up with my head resting in my palm. I stroked Lizzie, who was hunkered down beside me, watching Sophia pace up and down the bedroom.

Her hands were clasped behind her back, like a military general.

She was making me dizzy.

I have to admit I was quite surprised at the sudden change in Sophia. She was always a headstrong girl growing up, but I had never seen her this determined. It was like a light switch flicked on inside her.

Maybe she felt she was to blame for the malevolent bird, given that she was responsible for bringing it into the house?

After Mom left for her shift, I quickly bundled the bird into the garage, locking the door on my way back out.

There wasn't a peep out of the bird. But on that short walk to the garage I could feel its black beady eyes boring into me. Accusing me. It knew I tried to get rid of it and I don't think it was happy.

So here we were, a number of hours later, brainstorming new ways of getting rid of it once and for all. We discussed releasing it into the wild. Dumping the cage into the thrash. Even leaving it on an unsuspecting neighbour's front porch. Yet, every scheme we came up with had obvious flaws in it and we were starting to get frustrated.

Sophia was considering my latest idea and I could tell by the way her eyes narrowed that she was far from impressed.

"So, let me get this straight – you want us to just march back to that sanctuary place like 'sorry Mr whatever-your-name-is, we don't want your evil bird anymore. It eats snakes and we're afraid it might eat us next. Thanks anyway.'"

When she put it like that, my idea sounded ludicrous... almost as bad as leaving the cage on a neighbour's porch.

But what other options did we have? Mom would never believe us. We couldn't call Dad. Bob, the animal-loving caretaker, couldn't help us. It was only a matter of time before the bird caused more mischief. Which meant it was only a matter of time until I got in more trouble.

Maybe Mr Schimmel would take the bird back? Or we could just leave it there and hope he didn't notice. A tiny bird would blend in unnoticeably among all of the wildlife at his sanctuary.

I was about to respond to Sophia when a loud crash outside made us both jump. We ran to my bedroom window and looked out onto the backyard twilight.

"Hey! The garage door!" Sophia cried, pointing to the heavy garage door lying on the grass, ripped from its hinges.

A strong wind was picking up outside. It whistled

in and around the windows.

"No way is that wind strong enough to rip the garage door off like that," I said to Sophia, biting down on my lip. "It must weigh a ton!"

"Then what did, Archie? Don't tell me you think the bird done this?" she said incredulously.

I tried not to think of the possibility that the bird was getting stronger... more dangerous.

"Look I have a plan. We will strap the cage to one of our bikes and cycle to the sanctuary. Then, we will sneak in and leave the bird somewhere inconspicuous."

"Ooo big word, Arch."

"He might not even notice we returned it?" I said, ignoring the jibe. "And besides, even if he does figure out we returned it, he won't know where we live. Then, we sneak back out and make our way home before Mrs Parkinson checks in."

"But—" Sophia tried to interject but I was on a roll and didn't let her.

"When Mom or Dad ask about the bird, we say someone must have broken in and ripped the door off in the process. And the same burglar took Trevor! The perfect plan!" I cried enthusiastically.

"But Arch, you're forgetting one very important detail…" Sophia said with her arms crossed.

"…we don't know *how* to get to the sanctuary!"

The air went out of my sails like a deflated balloon. She was right. My brilliant plan, so carefully constructed, had a major flaw in it.

Above the whistling of the wind, a sound reached us. A faint but menacing note we knew all too well.

Chirp.

Did Mr Schimmel's sanctuary have a name? Where was it? Did Dad mention it before? How far was it from our house?

Important questions that I had no answers to. We tried searching online using my phone (Sophia's was still smashed up) but the world wide web was either drawing blanks or did not know that the creepy sanctuary existed.

And so, we found ourselves out in the backyard zoo, shivering and looking for clues. I draped warm blankets over the rabbit and hamster cages, given the nasty chill that was present throughout the room, blowing in from the now bare doorway. I didn't want them to freeze to death. The fish were fine in their heated tanks, as was Matilda in her heated enclosure.

The parakeet sat quietly on its resting spot on the table. I didn't think it deserved a blanket after all the trouble it was causing us.

Yet again, the yellow-feathered beast perched silently. Taking our measure. Why couldn't it behave like a normal bird should? Any squawking regular bird noise would have been preferable to the ominous silence coming from the cage. But this was no normal bird. We had established that much.

We checked loose papers and files, hoping to find something that would point us in the right direction. A leaflet, a written note from Dad... anything!

My eyes were drawn to the empty snake enclosure as I painfully remembered the horrible events of last night. Poor Trevor!

How is Dad going to take the missing snake news? I thought glumly.

"Argh it's no use!" Sophia shouted as she pounded the ground angrily. She was on her knees among piles of papers and files. "We're never going to get rid of this thing!" she sobbed.

I wanted to comfort her. To tell her that it would all be OK. Just like a big brother should.

But any hope I had was ebbing away like a rapidly receding tide. Maybe Sophia was right and we were stuck with the bird forever. Slaves to its will.

Suddenly, a scratching, shuffling sound made us both jump to our feet in panic. Something had entered the garage and was moving steadily in our direction. Panting heavily... excitedly.

"Buster! How did you get out of the house?" I said, relieved that it was the family dog and not some other monster.

Buster snorted happily and bounded forward, keen to slobber all over me like he always did.

"Whoops, I might have left the back door open," Sophia said. She didn't seem too sorry.

"Gerrrr-offf me Buster, your breath stinks!" I

shoved the excited dog away, wiping dog saliva off my face. It was hot and sticky. Disgusting!

I pushed Buster away so that he was now facing the birdcage. And out of nowhere, his demeanour changed. His body went upright and stiff, tail erect and rigid. He uttered a low growl, eyes locked on the birdcage.

Without warning, he bounded towards the cage and leaped into the air, paws outstretched.

CRAAAASH.

The dog collided heavily into the cage, knocking it to the dirt floor. It made a loud clanging sound as it hit the hard ground.

The previously silent bird was now squawking at the top of its lungs as it fluttered around the upside-down cage. I hastily covered my ears with my hands, trying to block out the painful screeching.

Buster also seemed to be affected by the noise, he stumbled backwards and trotted out of the garage, no longer interested.

I hurriedly picked up the cage, setting it upright on the paint-chipped table. The parakeet stopped screeching. It returned to its perch. And continued its vigil of staring at me with those midnight eyes. All was still in the backyard zoo again.

"Phew, not sure how much longer my ears could have taken that screeching."

"Archie - the cage!" Sophia shouted, pointing towards the birdcage.

"Huh? What am I looking at?"

"No! Underneath the cage! I'm sure I seen something on the base, markings or writing – maybe it's a clue!"

I tilted the cage slightly to the side. Sophia was right. On the base of the birdcage appeared to be some sort of writing or engraving.

I knelt down to inspect. I could just about make out an almost faded inscription:

HERSHEL WEBLEY

CLARKES LODGE

"Clarkes Lodge... Clarkes Lodge... why does that sound familiar?" I furrowed my brow in deep thought. "Not sure what Hershel Webley means but I've definitely heard of Clarkes Lodge before..."

"Wait – didn't Dad say we have to pass Clarkes forest to get to the sanctuary?" Sophia exclaimed.

"Soph, you're a genius!" I made to embrace her in a hug but she jumped out of the way.

"Not too close, don't want to catch *dorkitis*," she said playfully.

"Real mature. Anyway, I think I know how to get to Clarkes forest. I cycled there with Mom a couple of summers ago. If I remember correctly, it's a pretty long distance, so we need to be prepared."

"Prepared? What do you mean by prepared, animal boy?"

"You know, winter coats, energy bars for the

journey, tyres pumped, flashlights... oh, and some rope... and don't call me animal boy"

"Rope? For what?"

"How else are we going to lug that birdcage from here to there? I mean, look at the size of the thing! I'll have to take Mom's bike. It has a large basket in the front. We can use the rope to fasten the birdcage tight to the basket."

"You better pray none of my friends see us cycling around with that thing!"

I rolled my eyes. How was that even a concern at this point?

"It's dark and cold. I'm sure we won't bump into any of your cackling brigade, Soph. It's not like we have to cut through the mall. Now meet me outside in ten minutes."

Were we really about to travel in the dark, bitter coldness to the one place we knew wasn't safe? Would Mr Schimmel be waiting for us?

Inhaling a deep breath, I pushed these awful thoughts to the back of my mind and prepared for the journey ahead.

"All systems are go!" I cried as I sat on the adjusted saddle of Mom's purple bike. The oversized wicker basket at the front was laden down with the bulky birdcage – which was so big it only fit in at an angle.

I tied an old rope around the wicker basket and birdcage in an attempt to fasten it more securely.

Sophia had mounted her Raleigh Chic bike behind me. It looked brand new. My sister wasn't the outdoorsy type. In fact, I could only remember her out cycling on it once – the day it was bought for her!

She was wrapped in a light pink jacket with pink leggings and pink beanie hat, all matching the colour of the bike of course.

I, on the other hand, was a regular Bear Grylls when it came to the outdoors. During my brief spell as a boy scout, I achieved the merit badge for wilderness survival. I knew that would come in handy one day!

I was clothed in my khaki explorers' jacket and rainproof trousers. On my back was an army camo backpack that contained all essentials: energy bars, a torch, a magnifying glass (you never know) and Lizzie who was nestled in a side pouch. I thought about leaving Lizzie at home but having her with me made me feel a little less alone.

"Ready?" I called back to Sophia.

"Let's just get this over with," she shouted back.

"What?" I struggled to hear her over the howling of the night wind.

She gave me a thumbs up motion, gesturing that she was ready to go.

I began to wheel the bike around the side of the house but stopped in my tracks. Sophia's bike bumped into the back of mine. I quickly raised a finger to my lips in a shushing gesture before Sophia could tell me off.

Someone was knocking on our front door. I could hear the faint rapping over the swirling wind.

Carefully peering around the corner, I spotted old Mrs Parkinson hunched in the front porch. We couldn't afford for her to see us or else the whole plan would be ruined. She wouldn't hesitate to immediately call Mom if she knew we were sneaking out at night.

Quickly and silently, we rolled our bikes down the driveway and onto the street. The whistling wind may have muffled our escape or else maybe Mrs Parkinson was a little short of hearing lately, either way, we were speeding up the road and into the night. Hopefully she thought we were in bed, asleep. Too late to turn back now.

*****

The brisk night air chilled my exposed hands as they gripped the handlebars tightly. My lower back ached from straining to see over the protruding birdcage and ensuring I didn't crash into anything.

The wind rushed directly into our faces, almost as if it wanted to push us back home and away from the danger we were heading towards.

We cycled and peddled and cycled some more. Up and down hills and across busy streets until our legs burned. Leaving the residential neighbourhoods and business districts behind, we became very aware of the sudden emptiness of the city outskirts.

Out here we wouldn't find people chattering or cars honking their horns – no usual hum of a city. Only silence.

There were no lampposts to light the way. The only light came from a full moon, high in the night sky like a giant silver orb. Without it, we would be cycling into total darkness.

I skidded to a halt as we approached the giant billboard that represented the city limits. Sophia pulled up alongside me, panting heavily from the exertion. If we made it out of this in one piece, we both needed to exercise more.

"Why... did... we... stop?" she asked in between sucking deep lungfuls of air. She massaged her legs gently, trying to loosen them out after the long cycle.

"Well first of all, I think we both needed a break, and secondly, I can't remember what turn Dad took after this sign," I said, scratching my head and looking at the two different paths. One continued straight ahead while the other veered off to the right.

"You *said* you knew the way, Archie, don't tell me you made us cycle all the way out here and now we're lost!" she cried despairingly, stamping a pink sneaker on the ground.

"Calm down, we aren't lost. I just don't know which path to take. You see those trees?" I pointed beyond the two paths. "That's Clarkes Forest. We know that the sanctuary is somewhere near there. I think we could save a lot of time if we cut through—"

"Woah woah woah... you want me to go into a creepy forest... in the DARK?"

"I have a torch. And besides, do you want to make it home before Mrs Parkinson realises we're gone and calls the police or worse, Mom?"

She bowed her head in concentration and let out a deep breath. "I'll go in there on one condition... you give me your iPhone after all this is done? Don't think I've forgotten about last night!"

I smacked my forehead in disbelief.

"Fine, you can have the stupid phone. Now, can we go?"

We climbed into an empty field, carefully hoisting the bikes (and our yellow quarry) over the wooden fence that lined the road.

I gazed at the dark forest, peddling nearer to the shadowy blackness of its depths.

An inner voice told me this was crazy. That cycling into a dark, wild forest was madness. Dangerous on its own without having an eerie, wicked bird for company.

Despite my natural instinct to flee from possible danger, I ignored the inner voice.

Why didn't I listen to the inner voice?

We left the pale moonlit field and entered a world of shadows. Branches from the tall trees stuck out like deformed limbs, swaying back and forth in the howling wind.

After trudging a few yards into the forest, we were forced to dismount from our bikes and walk, such was the closeness of the thick tree trunks.

The path was uneven and sloped at awkward angles – a sure-fire way to break an ankle if you weren't careful.

Another few yards deeper and we were practically walking in pitch-black.

"I don't like this... I don't like this at all," Sophia whimpered.

The scant light that was afforded by the silvery moon was completely blocked out due to the high density of branches overhead. The deeper we went, the more distant the sounds of the wind became. I could vaguely hear it now but it seemed so far away.

I rummaged in my backpack.

"Ah-ha, Archie to the rescue," I said, pulling out the torch and illuminating the path ahead with yellow light.

"Maybe we should just go back to the main road?" Sophia begged, her fear by no means eased by the torchlight.

"Even if we did go back, we have no clue which path to take. If we take the wrong one, we could still be looking for this sanctuary come morning. And besides, I can't remember how to get back to the road," I said, cleaning my glasses on my jacket.

Sophia glanced nervously to the left, then to the right and finally behind. Her eyes took in the closeness of the trees and branches and the never-ending blackness. I could see her face grow paler by the torchlight.

"I wanna go home now! This was a stupid plan! Why did I listen to you in the first place?" I looked on, waiting for the tantrum to pass as it always did.

Before she could finish listing out a number of not so nice words to describe me, she was stopped in her tracks by a sudden rustling.

I heard it too.

But where was it coming from?

Somewhere in the dark undergrowth.

There it was again. A soft rustling or scratching, coming from someplace ahead.

Somewhere close.

Was there someone or something following us in the dark forest?

I shone the yellow beam from the torch in the direction of the noise.

Sophia's eyes were big and as wide as a terrified deer.

Another rustling. This time in a different direction. Off to the left. No, the right. I wasn't sure.

The light quivered as it darted from side to side. I was trying to pinpoint the exact location of the disturbance. I didn't realise I was shaking so badly.

A drop of cold sweat ran down my spine as I recalled every horror film I have seen involving dark nights in the woods. There was always some beast or creature lurking in the shadows, waiting for its unsuspecting prey. It never ended well for the poor lost kid in the forest!

What if it was a werewolf? It was a full moon tonight after all.

Get a grip, Archie, I told myself. *There is no such thing as werewolves.*

Then that annoying inner voice spoke up.

But... on the other hand, there is no such a thing as an evil parakeet yet exhibit A in the birdcage there suggests otherwise.

Shut up inner voice.

I felt Sophia cower close to me. I had to be brave. I was, after all, a big brother. And big brothers have to look out for little sisters.

"Who... who's there?" I managed to choke out.

Silence. Even the wind outside seemed to hold its breath.

"Show yourself, we aren't afraid!" I said, a little more bravely now.

I almost jumped out of my skin when I heard leaves crackling only a few yards from where I stood.

Something big was coming through the thick scrub. It was almost upon us.

Crunch. Crunch. Crunch.

Sophia was whimpering softly and muttering to herself.

I aimed the light into the darkness. A pair of menacing red eyes stared back at me.

"Oh nooooooooooooo!" Sophia screamed at the top of her lungs. It was so loud and shrill that I had to cover my ears, dropping the torch in the process.

"Ouch! You nearly burst my eardrum! What are you screaming at, Soph? Look, there's nothing to be afraid of."

A small grey squirrel shuffled out from behind a patch of weeds. It was nibbling on a chestnut innocently.

It wasn't a monster, or a werewolf, or anything scary. Just a squirrel.

Phew! I really need to get my imagination under control.

"Didn't I tell you there's nothing to be afraid of?" I picked up the torch. "It was only a squirrel."

Sophia didn't reply.

"Am I right, Soph? Sophia?"

I turned around and the first thing I noticed was Sophia's bike lying on its side. I spun in a circle, peering into the blackness for any sign of my sister. I cupped my hands around my mouth, calling out to her desperately.

No response.

Sophia was gone.

Fear crept over me like some hungry beast. The reality of my situation hit home.

I was alone in the woods.

Just like in every classic horror flick, I thought wryly.

"Sophia! Where are you? You better not be messing around!" I shouted, half hoping that she was playing a trick on me. In fairness, she had a track record in taking advantage of my naivety at the best of times.

Yet, as I clambered deeper into the forest, searching in vain for my missing sister, I couldn't shake the nagging feeling that this wasn't a trick. Sophia was in trouble. Don't ask me how but I knew it. Call it sibling intuition if you will.

I wasn't sure what direction I was walking in anymore. That grey rotted tree stump on my right looked awfully familiar. Everything looked the same. Skyscraper creaking trees and crunching twigs. Shadowy guardians of the wood.

I'm walking in circles. Great!

I couldn't recall the last time I had a panic attack but my anxiety levels were rising by the minute and I could hear my heartbeat thud irregularly.

Breathe, Archie, just breathe.

It was difficult to remain calm. I wanted to scream for help but knew it would be futile. A lesson from science class sprung to mind where Mr Laporte asked us 'if a tree falls in a forest and no one is around to hear it, does it make a sound?'

At the time, I didn't know what he was rambling on about but I think I understand now.

Sophia was right, I reflected. *This was a bad idea. We had a one in two chance of picking the right path out on the road where it was safe. We would probably be at the sanctuary by now!*

Thinking of the sanctuary, I looked to the wicker basket as I pushed both bikes up a steep slope, panting from the effort.

The bird had not made a sound since we left the house. It continued to watch me in silence, no doubt enjoying the predicament I was in.

I was keen to be rid of it once and for all. But first, I had to find Sophia.

An owl hooted somewhere high above. Probably out hunting like most nocturnal creatures. It must have a good view from up there. A bird's-eye view if you were high enough.

And that's when I got the idea.

I would climb as high as I could, where the branches grew thinner, and hope that I could spot Sophia. It was a longshot but it was the best idea I could come up with at this point in time.

Branches whipped and scratched at me as I clambered up the nearest mossy pine. I climbed higher and higher, each step more treacherous than the last. A quick glance down made me distinctly aware that one slip and I was done for! It was a long, long way to the cold hard ground.

Sticky bark lined my hands like a strong glue. Inconvenient and disgusting, but ironically might come in use if I were to lose my footing.

My head poked through a gap just as the limbs of the pine spread too thinly to support my weight. Clarkes forest spanned out around and below me.

"Where are you, Sophia?" I muttered quietly.

The top of the pine tree swayed dangerously in the wind. This far up, I was exposed and received no protection from the harsh elements. Every gust of wind stung my face bitterly.

I surveyed the dark forest, hoping against hope for a sign of my sister.

Wait! I spotted something. In a clearing not one hundred yards from the tree I was precariously perched on.

A flash of movement and a flash of pink. It had to be her!

One careful step at a time, I shimmied down the tree, hands sticking to the rough bark.

Grabbing the handlebars of both bikes, I hurried in the direction of the clearing, torch between my teeth. Fighting my way through a sea of weeds, thorns and thick roots, I pushed on in the near blackness.

Why did Sophia run off? How will I get rid of this blasted bird? How much trouble will I be in once Mom realises we snuck out?

So many questions weighed on my mind but I had to remain focussed. And I had to focus very hard to keep the torch between my teeth, balance the two bikes and ensure I didn't run head first into a tree.

At last, the clearing came into view. It was the first part of the forest I encountered that wasn't choked with tightly packed trees and shrubbery.

Pale light from the moon escaped down into the clearing, giving the area an eerie glow that was at odds with the surrounding blackness of Clarkes forest.

Approaching the clearing, I heard a sort of whimpering mixed with quick high-pitched chattering. I stopped in my tracks, carefully placing the bikes on the ground. Ever so quietly, I crept behind a nearby large bush.

Craning my neck, I peered behind the bush and my heart leapt. It was Sophia! There she stood in the middle of the clearing, unmistakable in her all-pink getup.

"Soph—" I started but stopped mid-call. Something was wrong here.

I could see my sister's face clearly now in the moonlight, and it was twisted with fear.

She cannot still be freaking out over that squirrel!

As I began to edge closer, I noticed something else. Sophia would dart one way, then stop abruptly. Before doing the same thing in another direction. Like she couldn't decide what way she wanted to go. That, or else something was blocking her path.

"Go away... leave me alone!" I heard her shout, in between sobs.

I couldn't see who or what she was shouting at. I needed to get a closer look before barging in there with no plan.

Switching off the torch, I tucked it into my backpack and lowered myself flat to the ground. Assuming an army-like position, I began to crawl. Dry crusty leaves lined the floor, ready to give away my location.

Last week, I watched an Animal Planet documentary on tigers. When stalking their prey, they would crawl silently, moving with the wind to mask their movements.

So, I behaved like a hunting tiger, waiting for the noisy whistle of the wind before gaining ground under some prickly bushes.

I ignored the many legged bugs that ran across my arms and legs as I disturbed their underground nests. Luckily, bugs didn't creep me out at all.

Finally, I reached the edge of the clearing.

"No way!" I mouthed in astonishment.

Sophia was surrounded by none other than a cute herd of bunny rabbits! Fluffy, adorable, white, grey bunny rabbits!

Only Sophia would be scared of bunnies, I thought.

As I inched forward, my elbow landed on a branch, cracking it loudly. The twelve or so rabbits jerked their heads in my direction. A scream caught in my throat.

The cute little bunny rabbits had long sharp fangs and razor-sharp claws – like mini Wolverines!

My attempt at mimicking the hunting tiger failed as twelve pairs of glowing red eyes locked onto me and hopped hungrily in my direction.

I couldn't believe what I was seeing. I didn't want to believe. It was like something straight out of a crazy nightmare.

Surely my mind was playing tricks on me? That dodgeball to the head probably just scrambled my brains around... yes, that was it.

I closed my eyes, pinched my arm forcefully and opened my eyes again.

I didn't wake up. I wasn't dreaming.

The terrifying balls of fluff were getting closer to my hiding place. I could hear them snarling and gnashing their fangs.

Out of the corner of my eye, I witnessed a number of them fanning out in a semi-circle position. They were taking up a flanking formation! Like a coordinated pack of hungry wolves.

Carrots and lettuce wouldn't satisfy these rabbits. No, these furry guys had a different menu in mind. And right now, I was the main course.

I had to do something before I was surrounded and trapped. Jumping to my feet, I issued a roar – my own version of a battle cry – challenging the fanged bunnies to face me.

My body shook with adrenaline as Sophia watched on, a look of shock on her face.

It worked. The bunnies stopped in their tracks. My war cry must have made them think twice about their choice for Tuesday night's dinner.

The herd of rabbits, a dozen strong, huddled together. Remarkably, it appeared as if they were conversing together. I could hear strange squealing and yelping noises. Since when did rabbits communicate like this?

Brushing dirt, twigs and bugs off my khaki explorer gear, I made to move towards my sister on the far side of the clearing, past the huddled bunnies.

But at that moment, they stopped what they were doing. They had finished their bunny discussion and it looked as if they had made a decision.

Growling menacingly, long ears stiff as boards, they slowly hopped in my direction.

Hop. Hop. Hop.

Picking up pace the closer they got.

I couldn't help but admire their shiny fangs as they caught the moonlight. Curved like the prehistoric sabre-toothed tiger and sharp as a butcher's knife. I didn't have time to investigate their elongated claws as I did the only thing I could think of at this point in time – I ran for my life!

The rabid rabbits snarled as they pursued me, slowly closing the gap to their next meal.

The pattering of their tiny feet on the dry leaves

came from all directions as I ran without a plan. Branches whipped my face, drawing small lines of blood in their wake. "Yeooowww," I yelled as I stubbed my toe on an exposed tree root, sticking up from the hard ground.

Limping on one leg, I made it a further ten yards before crashing to the ground in a heap, glasses flying from my nose for what must have been the tenth time in the past week.

Spitting out a mouthful of dry dirt, I glanced painfully to the side and recognised my surroundings. The camo backpack rested against a tree to my left beside Mom's bike. The bird cocked its head in my direction from its vantage point in the wicker basket.

Evil birds and mutant bunnies – what was going on here?

I reached for my glasses as the scurrying came to a stop. Although I couldn't see clearly, I could feel eyes on me. Hungry eyes.

My pulse quickened.

My heart thumped. Ready to jump right out of my chest.

Easing my blinkers on, I squinted into the darkness and groaned.

I was surrounded. Burning coal-red eyes leered at me in the dark from all angles.

Hop.

They tightened the circle.

Hop.

Closer now. I could see their fangs clearly now, razor

sharp instruments. Excellent for tearing into flesh.

I looked around desperately for anything that could be of use. Any weapon that might help me defend myself or at least put up one last fight before I became rabbit bait.

The rabbits purred and hissed, clicking their fangs together in anticipation.

Running out of options and time, I grabbed the backpack and rummaged through the contents desperately.

"Come on, come on... there's *got* to be something in here... ah-ha!"

I pulled out an energy bar. But not just any energy bar, a carrot flavoured energy bar!

"Look guys, I have something for you. You love carrots, right? Of course you do. Well, here's the next best thing – a carrot-infused protein bar! Excellent for muscle repair and err... good fang health?"

The bunnies stopped their advancements and sniffed the air suspiciously.

"Here you GO!" I shouted, throwing the energy bar as far as I could (which wasn't very far).

They didn't budge. The plan failed. I closed my eyes in defeat, waiting to be mobbed.

But when no attack came, I lifted one eyelid and was amazed at what I saw.

The bunnies had taken off in the direction of the energy bar. They clashed, bit, stomped and tore at each other as they fought over the carrot-flavoured treat.

It was like a bunny rabbit battle royale!

Sensing an opportunity, I quietly gathered up my backpack and pushed the two bikes in the direction of the clearing.

When I emerged from the bushes, Sophia was sitting with her back against a tree.

She was crying softly into her hands.

"It's OK now, Soph. I took care of it. They won't bother you again," I said, gently laying a hand on her shoulder.

Sophia lifted her watery eyed face and wiped the tears away.

"Sorry, Archie. I was so scared. I shouldn't have run away on you. I just panicked and next thing I knew I was surrounded by bunnies. But they weren't like normal bunnies and I was sure I was a goner!" she whimpered.

"Don't worry lil-sis, we're safe for now."

"Thanks," she sniffed. "And don't call me *lil-sis* ever again."

"Noted. Right so, onto the next problem – finding the sanctuary."

Sophia perked up suddenly.

"When I was trying to escape the bunnies earlier, I think I saw some smoke just over there," she pointed and continued: "Maybe from a fire or a chimney, I'm not sure."

"Let's check it out."

Leaving the clearing and mutant bunnies behind,

we plunged deeper into the woods, trusting that this terrible ordeal was nearly at an end.

We were in for a rude awakening.

The density of the woodland restricted any view of smoke or any signs of residence for that matter.

Guided by the torch, we wheeled our bikes in the general direction Sophia recalled seeing the smoke.

"Are you sure it was this way? What if the wind just happened to blow it this way and we're going in the wrong direction?"

Sophia turned on her heel and glared at me.

"My bad. Lead the way sis. After you."

After what felt like an hour – and in actual fact was only ten minutes – Sophia stopped. The darkness had a way of doing that. Time seemed to pass more slowly in here. It felt like we had been meandering through the forest for days.

"Why did you stop?" I asked.

"Can't you see that light? It's not very bright, but maybe it's coming from a house," Sophia said, pointing somewhere up ahead. "They could give us directions to the sanctuary."

Peering into the darkness, I spotted a dim glow in the distance. My instincts told me not to follow that light. But what other choice did we have?

We wheeled our bikes cautiously as we got closer to the source of the light.

What appeared to be an antique oil lamp sat atop a tree stump, illuminating the back of an old white cottage. The cottage was in an expanse of land flanked on all sides by thick trees. There were no paths leading in or out of the dwelling.

The white paint was chipped and blackened from years of neglect. Shoddy windows with broken panes lined up either side of a rickety screen door that banged in the wind.

Sophia echoed my thoughts out loud: "It doesn't look like anyone has lived here for a long while, Arch, let's keep looking."

I continued to examine the derelict cottage curiously.

"But then... who lit the lamp?" A chill crept down my spine as my imagination ran wild with thoughts of murderers and monsters lurking in the cottage.

"Let's keep searching for the sanctuary... I don't like the look of this place," I said, a sense of unease growing inside me.

Suddenly, a soft *plop* noise sounded behind me.

"Lizzie! Get back here!"

My scaly friend had somehow escaped from the pouch, dove onto a pile of leaves, scurried between my legs and was now making a beeline for the cottage.

"Lizzie! Lizzie!"

"She's done for, Arch, let's get out of here—"

"I'm not leaving her behind!" I fumed, dropping Mom's bike with total disregard for the caged bird –

who, very unbirdlike, didn't protest to the rough treatment – scrambling in my lizard's wake.

The reptile's tiny legs darted from side to side as it ventured towards the cottage. Why didn't I take her out of the pouch sooner? She hated being cooped up for long periods of time. My own fault for allowing her so much freedom.

I closed the gap to Lizzie, passing the flickering lamp on my way. I bent down low to scoop her up and—

Too late.

Lizzie disappeared into a tiny crack of a concrete structure jutting out from the back of the cottage. Upon closer inspection, I could see it was an old cellar.

Tugging hopefully at the rusted lock, I was surprised when it broke off easily in my hand. Then, grunting with the effort, I heaved open the wooden door.

"Oh no no no," Sophia said, shaking her head. "I'm not going down there."

"Fine by me. Well I'm going down here to get Lizzie. You can stay up here by yourself with the evil bird... alone. Oh, and hopefully those mutant bunnies aren't tracking your scent…"

Shadows from the oil lamp flickered in the billowing wind. Sophia eyes flitted from side to side.

"On second thought, maybe I'll stick with you."

"Wait, grab the birdcage."

Sophia stopped abruptly. "Why?"

"The only reason we're out here is to get rid of that

thing. I'm not letting it out of my sight. Besides, we're in enough trouble as it is. Dad will be fuming when he realises the backyard zoo is missing a snake! And can you imagine Mom when she finds out we left the house after dark?" I shuddered and this time it wasn't because of the chilly night air. "That ball of fluff is not coming back home to cause more trouble!"

For once, Sophia didn't argue. Maybe she understood that there was no going back at this stage as she half-carried, half-dragged the hefty birdcage.

"Now what?" She gasped for air at my side, wiping cold sweat off her forehead.

"Now, we go down."

We descended into another world of darkness.

I led the way as we balanced the birdcage between us, distributing the weight evenly. We had to be very careful with each step. I couldn't tell how far we were from reaching the bottom so slipping and falling would be a bad scenario.

The cellar's wooden stairs creaked and groaned, struggling to support us. Finally, we reached the cellar floor.

I wrinkled my nose at the damp stale odour that emanated from the basement. The moist air gave me a bout of goosebumps, sending cold shivers down my spine. I felt like I would never be warm again.

A clicking sound broke the silence.

It was only Sophia. She had grabbed the torchlight from my backpack, clicked it on and was now exploring the cramped cellar.

"Lizzie, where are you? No crickets for you

tonight if you don't come out now! I'm serious this time!"

"Ewwww," Sophia said from across the room. "Archie, look. Someone sleeps down here."

The torchlight illuminated a dirty bedspread in the corner of the basement. It was caked with mud.

"Disgusting! How could anyone live down here?" she asked.

But my attention was drawn elsewhere... to the plasterboard wall above the bedspread.

"Shine the light that way. Are those photos pinned on the wall?"

Sophia gasped loudly, a look of shock and horror painted on her face.

"Ar-Archie... why is your picture on the wall?"

I examined the polaroid closely, my heart beating against my chest. Sure enough, there I was, smiling in the picture. And it wasn't just the one picture either. The wall was lined with prints of me riding the school bus, in the school corridors... even looking out my bedroom window. They all looked pretty recent too. A chill ran down my neck as I tried to make sense of this creepy shrine.

"That's us outside the sanctuary on Sunday!" Sophia cried, pointing at a square picture.

"This is too weird," I said. "Who took those photos? And why?"

I scratched my head, confused at the wall of Archie in front of me in this dirty, dingy cellar.

"Well, some weirdo clearly seems to be a fan of you, Arch, and I'd rather not wait around for them to come back to their disgusting little house... so let's make like a banana and split—"

Sophia screamed hysterically as a dark shape brushed past her ankle.

"LIZZIE!"

I surged forward, a whisker away from grabbing the

117

darting Lizzie before she disappeared under a crack like a sliding envelope. Lifting my head, I realised it was a heavily scratched door and that Lizzie was probably somewhere in the room on the other side.

"Follow me!"

Sophia reluctantly followed me into the next room, dragging the silent bird in her wake.

"I can't see a thing! Pass me the torch," I said, extending my arm in Sophia's direction.

"No need," she said as she flicked a switch on the wall. A low hum of a generator vibrated. Overhead, shadeless light bulbs clicked into life, illuminating the room with a dim glow. Old cobwebs hung loosely from the ceiling like silver threads.

"What is this place?" Sophia asked. "It smells like our garage!"

Old, battered cages filled the otherwise empty room. I moved to inspect more closely and recoiled in shock when I noticed that some of the cages were not empty.

"Soph, there are animals in these cages!" Here's a bulldog... and there's a goat... and I think that's a guinea pig in the cage by the wall? Heya fella, you're a good boy, aren't you?"

The bulldog stood stiffly, eyes straight ahead, looking through me as if I wasn't there.

Sophia banged the side of the cage and clicked her fingers together. "Hellooooooo, anyone home? What's wrong with it?"

I moved to the next cage and studied the grizzled black goat. It looked familiar. Didn't I see this ram galloping wildly in the school gym earlier today? I couldn't be sure.

"I don't get it... it's like they're stuffed animals or something?"

"Not stuffed, Archie. Stuffed animals don't smell like this," Sophia said, pinching her nose.

"It's way too quiet in here... giving me the heebie jeebies."

Suddenly, I had a revelation. A light bulb over the head moment.

"What if this place is connected to Mr Schimmel's sanctuary?" I said excitedly. "What if, right now, we're under the sanctuary?"

"Take a chill pill, Arch—"

But I cut her off, I was on a roll, hopping animatedly on the spot.

"Yes, yes... it makes total sense. Think about it, Soph. The evil bird, the mutant rabbits and now the zombie animals down here? It's all connected! All connected!"

"Easy poindexter, don't bust a blood vessel. What are you saying exactly? That Mr Schimmel must be some sort of evil genius transforming innocent animals into supervillains?"

"I don't know what I'm saying but all I know is that this place must lead to Mr Schimmel's and we need to find the way in!"

Sophia rolled her eyes, looking unconvinced.

I ignored her and continued exploring the gloomy den.

"There must be a way... ah-ha!" I shouted, pointing at an opening in the wall at the very back of the room. It was almost hidden from view, partially blocked by an overturned rusty cage.

Shoving the blockage to one side, I stuck my head inside the opening.

"Hey! It's some sort of tunnel," I reported to Sophia. "Looks like it slopes upwards. I'd bet my life savings it leads to the sanctuary."

"You don't have any life savings. I know where you keep your piggy bank. Not even one dollar in there."

"Just grab the bird and give me the torch. It looks dark in here... and stay out of my piggy bank."

We squatted single file in the narrow tunnel. A fresh earthy smell filled my nostrils.

Sophia yelped as a wriggling worm fell on her head. It took her a whole minute to calm down.

We were forced to stoop as we began the climb along the newly dug passage, following the only light from the torch.

It was slow going in the tight space. My legs began to burn as the tunnel angled upwards.

Sophia was struggling to drag the birdcage up the sloping tunnel. I heard her mutter some not so nice words everytime it got snagged in the dirt or when she tripped over it.

After a number of energy-sapping minutes, a small sliver of white light appeared up ahead.

Yes! Finally, the end of the tunnel!

White light shone through the cracks of what appeared to be a panel covering the way out.

I carefully placed my hands on panel, testing the weight. Surprisingly, it slid effortlessly to the side.

Bright light stung my eyes. I could smell mould. It took me a few seconds to adjust after the darkness from the tunnel.

"What's up there? Is it the sanctuary? Let me see!" Sophia called impatiently from somewhere behind me.

"Shush, not so loud!" I whispered. "It looks like the storeroom?"

Food for every kind of animal lined the shelves. Supplies such as dog leads, kitty litter, chew toys, kennels and much more filled the brightly lit room.

I climbed out of the tunnel and helped Sophia out. I knew we were in the right place. Hoisting the birdcage, I headed for the door before Sophia stepped in front of me, blocking my path.

"Where do you think you're going?"

"To leave this guy beside the other birds."

"Why?" she demanded. "Let's just leave it right here and get out of this place!"

"You don't get it, maybe if we leave it beside the other birds, Mr Schimmel won't even notice we returned it?"

"That is *so* stupid. The plan was to get to the sanctuary and drop the bird. We're now *clearly* in the sanctuary. Hashtag, job done. I want to go home for a shower, I'm covered in mud! Now, give it here."

A game of tug and war ensued. Sophia pulled on the bird cage. I yanked harder.

Sophia lost her grip, tumbled backwards and knocked over a large fish bowl.

CRASH!

The clamour of the broken glass echoed throughout the room. We looked at each other, eyes wide with fright.

Did we just alert Mr Schimmel to our arrival?

I stood rooted to the spot, like a rabbit caught in the headlights of an oncoming truck. Sweat poured down my body.

I tried to stay as still as possible, focussing my attention on a shelf full of ripe bananas and assorted fruit. Probably for the veteran chimp.

Straining my ears, I listened for the inevitable sound of approaching footsteps but it was difficult to hear anything with the noise of my pulse pounding inside my head.

We stood there for what felt like hours. Afraid to move. Waiting to be caught.

Sophia looked ready to bolt at any moment. Raising both hands in a calming gesture, I indicated that we were safe. And let out a long breath of air.

"Phew! That was a close one. I don't think anyone heard us. Actually, come to think of it, maybe nobody is here? It must be past the opening hours. I mean, I've never heard of a twenty-four-hour sanctuary before," I said, chuckling nervously.

Sophia looked at me as if I were some crazy, escaped lunatic.

"When you're finished cracking yourself up, can we get on with this?" she said angrily, arms folded across her chest. "Incase you have forgotten, we just broke into a building and smashed it up. No way am I going to jail, Archie, I've my whole life ahead of me!"

"You won't be going to jail because we aren't going to get caught, OK?" I said, rolling up my sleeves.

I tried to sound confident. Truth was, I was more scared than I have ever been. I'm pretty sure I peed a little when the fish bowl smashed.

I looked at the yellow parakeet, wondering if it realised it was back home. It just stared back creepily, like it always did.

I hate this bird!

Grabbing the birdcage, I lugged it through the swinging double doors at the front of the storeroom. Sophia trudged along in my wake.

"We made it."

We stood near the rear of Mr Schimmel's sanctuary, illuminated by the bright blue fish tanks. Little and large tropical fish glided along peacefully, blissfully unaware of the dangerous world outside their watery homes.

I peered around nervously, looking for any signs of the creepy Mr Schimmel. The gnarled old chimp watched me impassively as I rounded a corner by his enclosure.

Glad I'm on the other side of that glass!

"Come on, the coast is clear," I whispered.

The sanctuary wasn't rowdy but it was by no means as quiet and eerie as the zombie animal room in the cellar. I felt more comfortable up here.

Passing a number of pens on my left, I couldn't help but notice that the inhabiting dogs behaved, well... normal. They wagged their tails and lolled their tongues happily. A pen of guinea pigs rustled among their shavings, content with their surroundings. Birds tweeted happily above my head, hanging from the ceiling in multiple cages.

I bet they don't eat snakes for dinner, I thought with a shudder.

Gazing up at the high ceiling again, I realised with a pang that there was no way I could get up there. I couldn't see any ladders either.

Sophia gave me the biggest 'I-told-you-so' stare. "So, now that your excellent plan of hiding the bird among the other birds is a no-go, we go with my plan."

"Which is…?" I asked, a little frustrated that my brilliant idea had come to nothing.

"We drop it like a hot potato, get out of here and never see this place again."

She snatched the birdcage from my arms and marched with conviction across the sanctuary floor. Balancing on the tips of her toes, she hoisted the heavy cage forward onto the countertop, so that it now rested beside the cash register. It left a jagged scrape on the work surface.

"Ta-da! Mission complete. Now, can we go?"

But she wasn't done yet. With a flourish, she pirouetted on the spot, one of her outstretched arms colliding heavily with the birdcage.

The cage rocked dangerously to the side as Sophia yelped in pain.

Right at that moment, the previously static, tongue-tied bird decided to go bonkers! It flapped its wings, rattling the cage from side to side. Sophia and I hastily covered our ears to block out the ear-splitting squawks.

"What's happening?" Sophia cried.

"I don't know! It must know we're getting rid of it once and for all," I shouted over the raucous screeching, "I don't think it wants to be back here."

"Well that's too bad, it's not coming back with us—"

An audible click coming from the direction of the front entrance grabbed our attention, putting an abrupt end to the discussion.

Someone was unlocking the door!

The bird stopped with its screeching and remained still.

Like it was trying to get the attention of its master!

I bolted for the storeroom just as the lock was removed and the heavy door pushed open, its creaking noise sending a shiver down my spine.

I rounded a corner at full speed, past a clan of gerbils munching on green leaves, knocking over a display of information leaflets titled SAVING OUR RAINFORESTS.

Re-entering the brightly lit storeroom, I looked around in a panic.

"Where is it?"

"Where is what?" Sophie asked from behind me, hands on her knees as she tried to catch her breath.

"The tunnel... i-i-it's gone!" I said despairingly.

I looked around wildly. Were we in the wrong room?

Nope.

Broken glass and gravel littered the floor, unmistakably from the accident with the fish bowl earlier. We were in the same storeroom all right.

But where was our way out?

I couldn't see any signs of the tunnel passage that led us into the sanctuary. It was as if it had disappeared, leaving no trace behind.

Approaching footsteps made a soft clip-clop sound.

We were minutes, maybe seconds away from being discovered.

"It's got to be somewhere here! Help me look!" I said desperately, searching the room hurriedly.

I inspected the walls, rubbing my hands zealously on the panels. Looking for a clue or any sign indicating a way out.

Sophia whimpered from somewhere behind me as she too struggled to find our escape route.

"It can't have just disappeared!" Frustration crept into my voice as panic started to set in.

I searched behind a large refrigerator, dotted with orangey-brown rust. A musty, pungent stench of mould greeted me. I gagged.

Yet, the foul odour jogged my memory. It reminded me of that stinky cheese Dad was so fond of.

"Hey! I think I found something!"

The palm of my right hand brushed against a narrow groove in one of the panels behind the refrigerator. The indent was practically invisible to the naked eye. Luckily, I have a great sense of smell. Not as good as a polar bear – they can smell a seal through three feet of ice – but good enough to recall the same mouldy odour when I first exited the dark tunnel.

Sophia rushed to my side.

"Hurry, Arch! We don't have long!"

Grunting with the effort, I dug my fingernails under the groove, pushing and pulling with all my might.

The pattering of footsteps from outside the storeroom were growing louder... and nearer.

"It's not moving!" I cried. "It's stuck!"

"Move, let me try," Sophia said, edging me out of the way.

She found the groove, frowning with concentration. The panel, flush to the wall, slid smoothly and effortlessly to the side, revealing the dark earthy tunnel and our route to freedom.

"Awesome, Soph!"

She smiled smugly. "See, told you I was more than just a pretty face—"

"I know you're in there, you won't escape..." a strange voice rasped. It was close. Too close for comfort.

"Quick! Get inside!" I urged.

We took off at breakneck speed into the surrounding darkness, bumping into the tunnel walls everytime the path meandered to the left or right. I didn't have time to retrieve the torch from my backpack. Right now, my only concern was putting as much distance between myself and the sanctuary.

I heard Sophia's laboured breathing from behind me as we crouch-ran blindly. I'd tell her to take a break but circumstances didn't allow that luxury.

Freedom was near. Faint traces of light appeared up ahead.

"Almost there, Soph, just a few more steps."

The end of the passageway was now clearly visible up ahead. Normally I wouldn't be excited about seeing a bizarre chamber of muted, zombie-like animals but life can be unpredictable.

I could taste freedom. A heavy weight had already left my shoulders from the minute we discarded the bird in the sanctuary.

I reflected on the trouble the evil bird had caused over the past number of days. From somehow opening all of the backyard zoo cages, to gobbling down a snake like a string of spaghetti and appearing in and around the school – it sure had done its damnedest to mess up my life and get me into trouble!

I was so relieved its days of troublemaking were over. Life could finally go back to normal.

The lump on my forehead throbbed as if in unison

with my thoughts, sending a painful reminder of the national championship's dodgeball match and worse, the outcome. School was not going to be fun tomorrow. Dylan Harrison had probably set a countdown timer to pound me into the ground. Maybe he would ease up if I told him all about the evil bird?

Nah, he would just punch harder.

But that was tomorrow's problem.

More importantly, the bird was out of our lives and wouldn't be troubling the Jones family again.

"I need a break... just let me stop for a couple of seconds," Sophia said between breaths.

Reaching behind, I grasped her hand gently.

"One last push, Soph, and we're out of here for good. I promise."

I pressed on and Sophia kept pace.

Finally exiting the tunnel passage, I entered the dim light of the musky room and collided headfirst into something solid that sent me sprawling on the hard ground.

Lying horizontal, I waited for my vision to come back into focus before glancing up curiously at a dark shape.

"Bob!"

Decked in his customary paint-flecked khaki overalls, stood Bob Hope, the friendly school caretaker and my friend.

"Boy am I glad to see you, Bob! You've *got* to help us!" I said, climbing to my feet, adjusting my glasses that sat twisted on my long nose. "We're being chased by this weird guy called Mr Schimmel; he owns the sanctuary at the end of the tunnel there. We think he is somehow turning animals evil. Like some hoodoo type stuff? We even got chased by mutant rabbits—"

"Easy, slow down now, Arch. Let's get you kids out of here. This isn't a place you should be hanging about." The caretaker's eyes appeared gaunt, like he hadn't slept for days. He turned on his heel and beckoned us forward.

I made to follow Bob out of the room but slowed down as my brain decided to start working. Sophia placed a hand on my arm, drawing my attention behind Bob's back. She looked nervous, suspicious.

Something didn't add up here.

"Hey Bob, quick question... how did you know we were down here?" I quizzed.

Bob stopped in his tracks.

He turned slowly. When his face came into view, he was smirking maliciously.

"Don't worry, Archie Jones. All will be revealed in due course."

Bob Hope, the helpful, animal-loving school caretaker, spoke confidently and without stammering, all traces of nervousness gone. The vacant, yet kind countenance I was so used to seeing had vanished. I was now looking at a different person.

"Now, let's play a game. The first part of the game involves you two crawling into those two charming cages right over there." He gestured towards two metal cages, vacant and lonely.

The cages stood in between two enclosures, one containing a badger and the other a turtle. Both animals stared straight ahead, neither moving.

"But... I don't understand? Bob, what's going on?" I was highly confused and a little afraid of the caretaker's new attitude.

"What's going on, my good fellow, is that you need to get into that cage. Pronto. Before I lose patience."

My heart froze. My stomach turned icy.

"No way am I getting into that thing!" Sophia said in disgust. "I can see mouse poop over there and... ewwwww, that deer just peed all over the floor!"

Bob made a gesture of impatience, massaging his

forehead with his index finger and thumb.

"You're not taking me seriously. I *hate* when I'm not taken seriously."

He gave a long low whistle and from the back of the room, the enormous wolf-like hound that nearly mauled me on my first visit to the sanctuary came plodding into view, lining up beside him.

The hound's eyes glowed an angry blood red.

"Now, are you going to get into the cage or would you like my friend here to escort you?"

Lowering its massive head, the wolf dog uttered a low, threatening growl, ready to attack at a moment's notice.

Sophia and I resignedly stomped towards the cages. Dropping onto our hands and knees, we crawled into the confined space. There was just about enough room for us to turn and face our captor as he slammed the doors shut, sliding bolt locks in place.

"Good! Just as I thought. Such smart kids."

Soiled straw, dirt and other disgusting filthiness stuck to my palms. Sophia was dry heaving in the cage next to me, the overpowering stench much stronger from a crawling position.

"I told you he was a weirdo!" Sophia muttered nasally from her cage. She was pinching her nose tightly to block out the odour.

"Bob, please, it's me... Archie! Why are you doing this—"

"Silence! And no more Bob this or Bob that! I'm done with that foolish guise."

"But... what do you mean? Who are you?" I asked, bewildered.

"You can refer to me as the Caretaker from here on out. Yes... the Caretaker." He chuckled heartily. "That will do splendidly!"

His greasy black hair glistened under the dim lights. Matted to his head, it gave him a slimy, unwashed look. Wild eyes, black as night, bore into me feverishly.

The Caretaker gave another low strange whistle and the large hound retreated to the back of the room. When it re-emerged, it was clasping something between its jaws, dutifully dropping the contents at the Caretaker's feet.

I identified the item as the Caretaker's notebook. The very same journal he carried around with him at all times. The one he used to keep a log on all of the animals he was studying.

The Caretaker carefully picked it up and oddly cradled it like a new-born baby.

I pushed repeatedly against the cage door. It gave slightly but then rattled against the heavy-duty bolt lock.

Snapping out of his reverie, the Caretaker's attention was drawn back to his prisoners. Us.

"I am quite fond of you, Archie Jones. You see, we are not so unalike, you and I. Both shunned by society for being different. Both more comfortable and accepted by other species we share the planet with. Outcasts because we don't fit the *mould*... mocked repeatedly and destined to be alone."

The Caretaker paused, a pained faraway look in his gaunt eyes. I looked on, confused, helpless and at a loss for words.

Words eventually came to me: "But Bob, err, I mean, *Caretaker*... what do you want with us? Why won't you let us go?"

"What do I want with you, you ask? Well, Archie Jones, I'm going to give you a choice. The offer of a lifetime you might say. Join me, as my assistant. Together, with an army of animal slaves, we can exact revenge on all of those who have wronged us!"

The feverish eyes of the Caretaker lit up with the enthusiasm of a preacher in mid-preach.

"Wait a minute, it was *you* who turned my bird crazy?" Sophia piped up as realisation dawned. "And those horrible mutant bunnies... that was you too?"

The Caretaker smiled proudly.

"Ah yes, I hope the bird didn't cause you too much trouble? One of my earlier experiments. And mind you, completely coincidental that it found its way into your hands. You see, I needed a place to work on my research and development. They chased me out of my last town – blasted animal activists! But if only they understood what my work was attempting to achieve!" The Caretaker's eyes burned with passion and hatred. "I couldn't believe my luck when I found an old broken-down cottage not one hundred yards from an animal sanctuary! The perfect place to work on my *pet* projects and test them out on the public. That old fool Schimmel was none the wiser. He accepted my projects without question and provided me with many test subjects, albeit, unknowingly. In fact, I must thank him – after all, he indirectly assisted in bringing you here to me, ahead of schedule."

My mind was spinning. I had been wrong about Mr Schimmel all along. He wasn't the bad guy here. In fact, he wasn't to blame at all. I had wrongfully assumed his odd behaviour and peculiar appearance were indications of wicked intent.

I judged a book by its cover. Something Mom told me never to do.

Mr Schimmel wasn't responsible for setting mutant, freak pets into Virginia Falls. That particular person now stood in front of me.

"I still don't get it; how did you turn my birdy evil?" Sophia asked.

"Ah, right on queue, Ms Jones. How about I show you?"

Again, he issued a low whistle and the wolf hound trotted out of view.

A distressed half-squeal, half-quack sounded from somewhere close. When the hound reappeared, it had something clamped between its jaws that struggled against its grip.

I spotted an orange beak and webbed feet.

"Pay attention while I add this unimpressive duck to my growing army of friends." He opened his journal and began to sift through the pages. Furrowing his brows in concentration so that they were almost joined, like a black hairy caterpillar, the Caretaker began speaking softly under his breath. His voice rose and fell. I could only catch some words but the more I listened, the more I was sure that something very wrong was happening.

The Caretaker shut his eyes as the chant came to an end. The duck stopped squirming and was let down gently by the hound. All looked normal until it opened its beak and belched a stream of fire that lit up the dim chamber.

The wave of blazing heat forced me as far back as I could go in the steel cell.

I felt a mixture of sickness and fear in the pit of my stomach.

The fire-breathing duck waddled obediently into an empty cage near me, eyes glowing red.

"Erm, Mr Caretaker, you mentioned you were going to give me a choice? What's my other option? The one where I don't join you in turning animals into slaves?" I asked, already afraid of what the answer might be.

The Caretaker shut the malevolent journal and smiled thinly.

"Ah yes, a choice. I'm glad you asked. I'm sure you realise, being such a smart child, that I can't just let you go now that you know my plans? Thus... refuse to join me, and you can be the first test subject of my newest experiment."

"Experiment? What experiment?" Sophia butted in.

The Caretaker ignored Sophia as if she wasn't there, keeping his eyes locked on me.

"I call it the *transfiguration experiment*. Mr Jones, how would you like to become the first human to be transformed into a rat?"

How would I like to be transformed into a rat?

Pure terror washed over me, raising the hairs on the back of my neck. My mouth ran dry. My mind whirred.

Surely it wasn't possible? Was the Caretaker capable of such a feat?

At this point, the improbable was possible. After all, I had just witnessed the power of the journal first-hand as the Caretaker added another innocent victim to his mutant army of slaves.

"I don't understand... why are you doing this? Why me?" I asked.

"I've been watching you very closely since I took up shop in Virginia Falls. Barely two months ago – my first day as caretaker in that dreadful place you call school – I watched you sit alone in the yard. The other kids ignored you. Your very own sister even pretended you weren't there! That day I witnessed a vision of my younger self in you. A kindred spirit if you will"—he absentmindedly caressed the head of the large hound—"and to my utter amazement I soon realised we shared the same passions." He raised his arms wide, gesturing at the room's animal occupants.

My head hurt. I was finding it extremely difficult to wrap my head around what was happening. All I knew was that my knees were aching painfully, I was trapped in a cage and apparently had a choice to either join the Caretaker or be transformed into a rat. On top of all this, I felt hurt and naive that I believed this man to be my friend.

"I'm sure you're wondering why I chose to place myself in Montgomery?"

I stared back blankly, at a loss for words.

"No? Well, let me tell you anyway while we're here. Your puny school was an excellent place for me to observe the habits of the children in Virginia Falls. I am strongly of the opinion that the best time to learn life lessons is pre-adolescence. Too many juvenile brats are left unchecked and inevitably turn into ignorant adults! Unlike the butterfly, metamorphosis gone terribly wrong!" Spittle flew from the Caretaker's foul mouth.

He continued: "My animal friends and I are going to teach the world a lesson, starting with Montgomery Elementary School. You witnessed my power first hand during your hare-brained dodgeball event today, no? That Dylan Harrison is a horrible excuse for a human being and needed to be taught a lesson! The look of pure terror on his face when my army attacked! That goat to your rear is still chewing on what's left of his Montgomery jersey."

"Wait, it was you who set those animals loose in the school?" I quizzed.

"Of course it was me. Do you not agree that it was necessary? That bullies like that need to be thought a lesson before they get worse? I know you're not the least bit fond of the Harrison boy? Can you now see what we can achieve together?"

The Caretaker's eyes dropped to the journal he held in his left hand.

"Join me, Archie Jones, and together we will rid the world of the insolent through our army of beastly slaves!"

I considered his vision. *Dylan Harrison deserved to be thought a lesson*, I thought. *And I'm fed up of always being picked on.*

Time seemed to slow down. The Caretaker's lair suddenly felt like it was miles away. Sophia was saying something to me but all noise was muffled, as if I was underwater. The Caretaker smiled widely, knowing that his powerful words were inciting a dark part of me that I didn't know existed.

Out of nowhere, a flash of purple came into my line of sight, charging into the Caretaker and sending him sprawling onto the hard dirt ground.

"Mr Schimmel!" I yelled, "Look out for the wolf-dog!"

But the formidable hound didn't attack. It was behaving as if it had just woken from a nap and wasn't entirely sure what was going on or where it was.

"It's not under the Caretaker's spell anymore," Sophia cried. "The tail is wagging!"

No longer under control, the hound moseyed off happily in the direction of the exit, past the limp body of its former overlord.

"Are you children hurt? I need to call the police,"

Mr Schimmel looked around the hideaway in disgust, clearly concerned for the wellbeing of all the captured animals, "but first, let me set you free."

"Mr Schimmel, that's our school caretaker, he's some sort of evil hypnotist. He's been turning animals into his slaves... transforming them into monsters... even sneaking them into your sanctuary!" I cried.

Mr Schimmel paused as he bent down to examine the bolt locks, concern written across his features.

Sophia spoke up: "Yeah, and his black magic mumbo jumbo is all in that journal he carries around! We thought—"

"You thought what? That this old crackpot could stop me?" The Caretaker, now back on his feet, dusted himself off and glared at the sanctuary owner.

"Is this true? What the children speak of?" Mr Schimmel asked.

"Children say such silly things I find. Anyway, do you like poetry, Mr Schimmel? Of course you do. Let me read you some of my latest work, I'm sure you will find it agreeable. Now, if only I could find the correct entry—"

"NO! Don't let him read from that!" I cried out.

Too late.

The Caretaker had begun chanting, the tone of his voice growing in power as he worked his dark magic. I struggled to make out the words but this incantation was certainly different from the last. More direct and commanding.

Mr Schimmel hesitated. Maybe curiosity got the better of him but he made no move to stop the

Caretaker.

A shutter banged from somewhere behind me, followed by a clip-clopping sound. A powerful black ram sauntered into view. It had long, curved horns, long dark hair and split hooves. Unnatural muscles rippled beneath its fur.

"What devilry is this?" Mr Schimmel asked, bewildered as the ram stared him down.

"Attack!" roared the Caretaker.

Eyes glowing ember red, the extraordinarily large ram lowered its head and charged, horns protruding dangerously.

"Oomph!" grunted Mr Schimmel as he was struck directly in the gut, walloping his head against a metal cage on his way to the ground. A wooden pipe fell from an inside pocket of the sanctuary owner's robe, shattering into two pieces.

I looked forlornly at our short-lived saviour, stretched out, unmoving in the dirt.

Out cold.

The Caretaker smirked wickedly. To my dismay, he reopened the malevolent journal.

"Let us out of here!" Sophia cried, her knuckles turning white as she gripped the cage tightly.

Mr Schimmel lay sprawled on the ground, a tangled mess of purple. His chest rose up and down slowly.

The ram was gone. It had served its masters purpose for now.

The Caretaker paced back and forth, arms behind his back, clutching the journal dearly.

The room was silent again, apart from the shuffling sounds of the Caretaker's pacing. I could feel my heart pounding in my ears. I tried to think clearly but it was proving difficult with the growing pain in my head, the constant aching in my knees and the physical and mental exhaustion I currently felt.

"So, Mr Jones. Here we are. You have witnessed the power I possess. Now for the million-dollar question, will you join me?"

A wave of nausea passed over me. I struggled to find words. There would be no happy ending here, no going back to an ordinary life.

What choice did I have other than to join the

Caretaker? I'm no hero. And becoming a rat was not an option. Out of the question. No chance.

"I'll ask you again, Archie Jones, will you be by my side? Will you use my growing army of slaves" – he gestured at the silent animals throughout the dim den – "to exact revenge on all those who have wronged you?"

Two trains of thought sped around my head. Figuratively speaking, the devil on my left shoulder whispered for me to join the Caretaker. To never let bullies like Dylan Harrison torment kids like me ever again. The kids at school would have no choice but to accept me as their new leader, Archie Animal Overlord Jones!

The angel on my right shoulder adopted a different approach, reminding me of my love for animals. How we share this planet with them as equals, not as slaves to do our bidding. I thought of Lizzie, my best friend... of Arnold, chewing his lettuce happily... of Trevor—

Anger coursed through me. It rose from the pit of my stomach, unbidden. In that very moment, it all became clear to me.

"Slaves? Servants?" I shouted from my cramped position, "We're nothing alike... and we never have been! I thought you were my friend, but you're nothing but a cruel, evil, LOSER! I'll never join you!"

The Caretaker tsk-tsked. "I had high hopes for you, Mr Jones. I thought we understood each other." He looked visibly disappointed as he inspected his dirty fingernails.

"Oh well," the Caretaker shrugged his shoulders,

sighing dramatically, "no use crying over spilt milk. Time to test the transfiguration experiment."

"Noooooo," Sophia wailed, "please don't turn my brother into a rat! I know he can be annoying and all but he's a real nice guy. And caring... I couldn't have asked for a better big brother!" Tears formed in her brown eyes.

"Charming," the Caretaker replied, "really, it is. You know, when you beg like that, you're strikingly familiar to a sea lion. Sophia the sea lion... do you like the sound of that?"

Sophia stopped sobbing as the reality of the Caretaker's threat sunk in.

"Now, where was I? Ah yes, time to unleash the rodent within!" He opened the journal, eyes ablaze.

"You're a sicko!" I shouted. Granted, not the cleverest insult I could have thrown at him but it was the best I could do at that moment.

The Caretaker found the page he was looking for in the dreaded journal and the horror began to unfold.

He started slow, speaking rapidly in undertones.

"STOP! Please just STOP!" Sophia roared from beside me.

The Caretaker's voice rose in pitch and volume.

"You're crazy—" I began but before I got the words out of my mouth, I felt a tingling all over. Like my whole body had developed pins and needles, only the pins were pricking my skin and the needles piercing my organs.

I cried out in alarm as discomfort turned into

searing pain.

Wincing through the burning agony, I felt something protrude from under my nose.

"Oh noooooooooo!"

Four long and hairy black whiskers twitched above my lip.

Evil laughter erupted from somewhere close.

Sophia screamed nearby.

"Oh no no NO!" I cried as my nose began to grow outwards, stretching my face tightly. I was developing a snout!

Panic set deep into my bones. Sweat dripped down my newly formed snout.

I was about to pass out. Never had I experienced fear such as this. I've loved being around animals for as long as I can remember, but never in my wildest dreams did I think I would ever become one!

Especially not the house pest rodent variety.

Something long, skinny and leathery brushed against the back of my knee. I slowly turned my head, eyes widening in terror at the furry grey tail sprouting from my backside.

I was seconds away from becoming a fully-fledged rat.

The pungent smell of nearby rotten meat filled my new nostrils. Ordinarily, this would have disgusted me. Cause me to be sick to my stomach. Rather, it made me... hungry! Like a ravenous jungle beast.

"HELLLLLP!" I wailed.

Yet, instead of mocking laughter, this time my ears – which had become pointy – heard cries of alarm. The cries didn't come from Sophia's cage – she was doubled over, hands covering her eyes, unable to watch my horrid transformation.

As quick as it came, the searing pain receded back to a faint pricking all over. Gradually opening my eyes, I was surprised to see my new snout casually transforming back into my usual long nose and the black whiskers dwindled before disappearing entirely. Swivelling my neck, waves of relief washed over me as the rodent tail was nowhere to be seen.

"Sophia!" I shouted, "I'm still me! I mean, I'm not a rat! It didn't work!"

Sophia slowly lifted her head, as if she was afraid of what she might see in the cage beside her.

Her complexion shifted considerably from sheer

terror to utter relief as she gazed upon the Archie she had grown up with... red, curly hair, long nose and a distinct lack of rat features.

More frantic cries swiftly drew our attention. The first thing I spotted was the journal. It lay lonely on the dirt floor, discoloured pages facing outwards.

But where was the Caretaker?

Further howls of discomfort echoed – coming from somewhere to the rear of the dark refuge – before the Caretaker came back into view.

"What's he doing?" Sophia asked, bewildered.

I looked on in a similar state of confusion as the Caretaker thrashed about like a bull in a china shop, careening into cages occupied by silent furry mammals, cold, unmoving reptiles and colourful immobile birds. His arms flailed about wildly, tearing at his overalls, as if he had a sudden itchiness that couldn't be scratched away.

Amidst the unexpected chaos, I looked for a means of escape. I pushed with all of my might against the cage door, panting with the effort. But the door clanged against the bolt and held firm.

Mr Schimmel groaned weakly. I peered hopefully at the sanctuary owner but it was clear he wasn't going to be moving anytime soon. A skinny wooden object lay half-concealed under the purple robe, almost camouflaged against the brown dirt laden ground.

"The pipe!" I exclaimed loudly.

"Huh?" Sophia said.

"If... only... I... can... reach... it."

After just about squeezing one skinny arm through the cage bars, I stretched towards the broken pipe. My fingertips brushed the wood, agonisingly close.

Sophia caught on and shouted words of encouragement. "Come on, Arch! You can do it…oh that was close! You definitely moved it there. Try again… Oh, unlucky!"

With a final grunt, ligaments strained to their maximum, shoulder ready to pop out of its socket, my fingers finally found purchase.

"Got it!"

Hands shaking with adrenaline fuelled hope, I poked the broken pipe through a narrow gap in the steel. After tinkering with the mechanism for a few seconds, an audible click sounded as the bolt slid upwards and the cage door flung open.

I was free.

"You did it! Now, GET ME OUT OF HERE!"

I hurriedly came to my sister's rescue, sliding back the bolt lock – which was much easier done on the outside – on the steel pen. Stretching the pains and aches out of our cramped muscles, we now stood awkwardly in the Caretaker's lair.

"What's happening to him?" Sophia asked. Her hair was dishevelled. Mud caked her clothes and face. I barely recognised my ordinarily prim and proper sister.

The Caretaker was doubled over, scratching at his left leg, near the ankle. Something small, fast and yellow with black leopard spots slid out of his overalls, coming to rest on the Caretaker's heavy boots.

"LIZZIE!" I shouted. "There you are!"

The Caretaker brought his right boot high and stomped down on his left foot in a mad effort to squish the tiny lizard. He howled in pain and frustration as the curious reptile scampered away to safety.

Sophia sniggered as the Caretaker hobbled to his feet. Not the most intelligent thing to do given the circumstances but, Sophia being Sophia, she couldn't help herself.

Immediately, the Caretaker's attention snapped back to his now escaped prisoners.

"Why are my two experiments out of their new homes? I thought we had an understanding? Was I not crystal clear before?" His cruel mouth grew so thin it nearly disappeared from sight. Anger burned behind his cold black eyes.

"Erm, Arch? What do we do?" Sophia stood in front of me, blocking me from view of the Caretaker.

"Yes Mr Jones, what *do* you do now? I'm sure you'll realise that you have run out of options. In a matter of minutes, you will have joined my ranks and will never see your parents or loved ones again. Well, unless I command you to nest in their home," he smirked threateningly, "oh how delightful that would be."

I made no effort to respond.

"Arch? Now would be a good time to run I think," Sophia said, not taking her eyes off the Caretaker.

"Mr Jones, what are you doing back there?" the Caretaker snapped.

Sophia stepped aside. The Caretaker's eyes widened, fright painted across his pale gaunt face for the first time.

For I was holding something in my hands. A black journal. The Caretaker's journal. The source of his power.

"Give that here, boy. Now!"

I had the journal open on a yellowed page, headed: TRANSFIGURATION - HOW TO TURN A HUMAN INTO A RAT. Under the heading, various crude drawings depicted the awful transformation process. Below the drawings, scrawled by an inky hand were a couple of paragraphs of text. These must be the lines the Caretaker uttered earlier. The spell that *almost* turned me into a rat. I started to read:

"Whiskers will help guide you,

As you burrow deep in the earth,

Beady are your black eyes,

Prepare for your re-birth—"

"How dare you speak those words, *my words*!" The Caretaker spat.

I ignored the outburst and continued:

"Squeezing in holes and cracks,

Fur as black as night,

Scavenging for a living,

A squeaking rodent sounds right—"

"I command you to stop, foolish boy! You know not the potential of what you hold in your infantile hands!" The Caretaker stood rooted to the spot. I finished:

"This spell grants me the power,

You just wait and see,

For life will change as you know it,

[Insert Name], a rat you will now be."

"Insert name? What does that mean?" Sophia said as she looked on expectantly.

"Hang on," realisation dawned on my pale face, "*Bob Hope*, a rat you will now be!" I shouted triumphantly.

"NOOOO! This... can't... be... happening!" The Caretaker's body convulsed. His eyes spun wildly in their sockets. He clutched his back in obvious pain.

And then, he started to laugh.

"You juvenile fools," he said mockingly, "my identity is unknown to you or anyone in this dismal town!"

The spell didn't work. I didn't know his true identity. Once again, the Caretaker was one step ahead. My last shred of hope left me like air escaping a punctured dodgeball.

"Now, my life's work in your *grubby* hands – give it here and let's get you both back into those cages. Quietly and without fuss, like good slaves."

"Cages…" I whispered under my breath. An idea began to take form in a corner of my mind. It was one of those ideas that you could only think up when all else was lost. A last chance saloon in idea form.

"Sophia, remember we knocked over the bird cage at home?" I said hurriedly.

"Er, yeah, but now is probably not the time to talk about that fight, Arch."

"No! I mean, when we knocked it over, there was a strange name underneath it right? Above Clarkes Lodge? Webber or something… Webley?" – the Caretaker's body went rigid – "Yes, that was it! But I can't remember the first name!"

The glimmer of hope was about to be extinguished when Sophia said cooly: "Hershel. That was it. Like the chocolate?"

In that moment, the Caretaker's manner wasn't confident. Neither was it as terrifying as it had been mere seconds before. It wasn't nervous or stuttery, like Bob Hope, either. Like a cornered rat, powerful waves of fear radiated from the Caretaker, almost strong enough to cause shimmers in the air.

"Archie, my boy. I've always been good to you, yes? We've been friends for some time now. Please pass me my journal and we can forget this ever happened."

The Caretaker's tone became soft, almost gentle. His oily skin glimmered in the dim light.

I looked once upon the pathetic, begging form of my one-time friend. And then I did what anyone in my situation would do. I started to read the spell again.

I spoke aloud the first verse.

"STOP! Please Archie," the Caretaker sobbed, "who will protect you against the vile bullies from here on out? Against the Dylan Harrison's of this world?"

Keen to drown out the false words from across the room, I shouted the second verse at the top of my lungs, much more confidently this time.

"You must stop! I must finish my work!" The Caretaker cried. "I will put an end to this myself!" The Caretaker started across the room menacingly, arms stretched out in front of him, closing the distance quickly.

Knowing I was seconds away from being strangled to death by this maniac, I looked around desperately for a weapon, grabbing the nearest object in sight. It appeared to be a circular bird cage... an odd shape... reminded me of a... dodgeball!

Using every last ounce of my ten seconds of dodgeball experience from earlier today, I flung the round cage as hard as I could.

BAM!

Direct hit! It struck the Caretaker's head, knocking him off-balance momentarily. But only momentarily. He got straight back to his feet.

And looked even angrier than before.

"Quick, Arch!" Sophia shouted. "Finish the spell!"

I felt a vibration run up my arms as I started on the last and final verse. It originated from the journal which now appeared to be a stronger, brighter version of yellow.

The Caretaker was almost on me.

But he was too late. I made it to the very last line of the spell.

"HERSHEL WEBLEY, A RAT YOU WILL NOW BE!"

The Caretaker stopped in his tracks, mere inches away from grabbing me. Long spindly arms slowly lowered by his sides. A vacant expression befell his face, as if he was daydreaming. He mouthed a silent "no" as long grey whiskers burst forth above his upper lip.

I looked away in disgust as the Caretaker's head began to shrink, beady black eyes starting to dwindle in their sockets. This was followed by a number of popping sounds amidst cries of pain and discomfort. And then silence.

"I think I'm gonna be sick," Sophia said.

Paint-flecked grey overalls lay discarded in a heap. They pulsed gently as something tried to claw its way out from the tangle. Orb-like black eyes appeared first. Followed by a long snout, sniffing the air suspiciously. The skinny black rat stood on its hind legs, staring at me.

Perhaps considering one final attack.

The once all-powerful Caretaker took one final look at me before turning swiftly and scampering across the room.

"Don't let him get away!" I shouted.

But the rat was fast. Its claws skittered across the dirt floor as it spotted an opening, a crack in the wall. It's ticket to freedom.

Hershel Webley, the rodent, was inches away from escaping when BANG!

A steel cage was thumped down over the rat, trapping it underneath.

"Sophia! You got him!" I said with delight.

"It was nothing," Sophia said, inspecting her nails casually, "I owed him one after what he did to my bird."

The morphed rat looked for a means of escape, gnawing on the steel mesh and running about wildly. All in vain. The Caretaker was captured.

A groan of pain from nearby reminded us that Mr Schimmel was still in the room. He hobbled over to us, holding his side in clear discomfort from the earlier collision with the ram.

His eyes lingered on the trapped rat before resting on me.

"I'll take that, Mr Jones," he said, pointing to the journal pinned under my armpit. "This book of *evil* is not safe. It must be destroyed before it falls into the wrong hands."

He didn't have to ask me twice. I was only too happy to hand the mouldy journal over.

"But—what about these guys?" I gestured towards the silent, abnormal occupants in the cages throughout the den. "Can we help them?"

"I admire your concern for the welfare of these trapped souls, Mr Jones. I promise I will consult this manual and look to reverse the damage that has been done, although I cannot say with certainty if it will be possible or not."

"What are you going to do with him?" I gestured towards the black rat, isolated and alone inside its new metal home.

"I'll think of something for our furry little friend, trust in me when I say he won't be causing anymore trouble for the rest of his life. Which incidentally is on average two years for your typical rodent."

The former Caretaker seemed to take this news very badly, thrashing recklessly against the metal prison.

Sophia tugged on my sleeve. "Erm Arch, we should probably start making our way home. Mom is probably freaking out by now and I'd rather not be grounded for the rest of my life."

"You children go on home; you have done a great service to Virginia Falls and to its animal world. Mr Jones, without you, who knows what evil deeds the Caretaker would have accomplished with his army of slaves. I hope you understand just how special you are."

I would have been thankful for the praise, even a little embarrassed, but I had never felt so tired in my life. I was just eager to get home.

Something pushed lightly against my foot. I looked down to see Lizzie gazing up at me. I carefully lifted the lizard, placing her inside my pocket.

"My sister's right, we should be going before our mom declares us missing," I added with a tired smile.

"You will always be welcome at my sanctuary. My gratitude runs deeper than you know. Farewell for now."

With that, we bade farewell to Mr Schimmel. I made a point not to look in the direction of the captured rat and former Caretaker – it would be too soon if I ever saw a rat again.

And so, with aching limbs and tired minds, we exited the Caretaker's lair the way we had come in. Through the filthy basement – where I made sure to tear down the creepy photos of myself – past the stained bedspread and up the creaking steps before emerging back into the closeness of the dark forest. The night was silent, other than the chirping of nearby crickets. The wind that had previously battered against the cottage was gone, as if the forest was inhaling a deep breath.

"Arch, erm…" Sophia started rather uncomfortably, "well, I just wanted to say, you were amazing tonight. We wouldn't have made it out of there if it wasn't for you."

Resting against a tall tree, I raised a curious eyebrow as Sophia continued, "I mean, I know I *sometimes* give you a hard time—"

This time I raised both eyebrows.

"—OK, I've been a total jerk to you recently, and

I'm sorry for that. I promise to be nicer from now on. I'll even start by cleaning up the backyard zoo when we get home."

I couldn't quite believe my ears. I couldn't remember the last time Sophia sent a compliment my way, or if I had ever gotten one from her at all. In fact, I couldn't remember the last time she had said something nice about me for that matter!

"Thanks Soph. But the backyard zoo part... I'll believe it when I see it," I said playfully.

"Come on, let's get out of here."

The homeward cycle was a lot more enjoyable than the journey we had taken only a few hours ago. We whooped and hollered and zig-zagged on the quiet roads. High fiving each other emphatically. The silver light from the pale full moon guided us in the direction of home.

I felt warm on the inside and considerably lighter, like a huge weight had been lifted from my chest.

We had defeated the Caretaker and ruined his evil plan. Because of us, there would be no animal slave army.

Virginia Falls was safe.

People would sing about our victory for years and years to come – if they only knew about it. And most importantly of all, I was fully human – most definitely not a rat.

I guess there are multiple lessons to take away from the sanctuary incident. 1) Don't judge a book by its cover – yes, Mr Schimmel looked every bit the bad guy but deep down he was just a caring, eccentric animal lover. 2) Always believe in yourself – a couple of days ago I would never have believed that I had it in me to defeat an evil villain and save Virginia Falls. 3) Stand up to bullies – sometimes a bully needs a whack to the head with a dodgeball to show them you aren't afraid. And 4) Don't trust a creepy, slimy caretaker who pretends to be your friend – I guess this one needs no explanation?

A short while later, we pulled our bikes around a corner and onto our street block. The neighbourhood slept, safe in their beds, blissfully unaware of what went down at Clarkes Lodge.

"Let's go in the back door, just in case Mom got home early and thinks we're in bed," I said as we peddled into the driveway.

"Good thinking, I feel like I could sleep for a week! I can barely keep my eyes open here," Sophia added.

Silently, we crept into the kitchen and proceeded to the living room on tiptoe.

"Soph, do you hear that?" I whispered, "uh-oh, I think Mom is home!"

We walked into the living room, expecting to see Mom, arms crossed and livid with us for leaving the house so late.

But instead, we came upon a different scene. A scene so frightening and utterly terrifying that it caused Sophia to scream and my jaw to hit the floor.

Perched on the mantelpiece, was the golden yellow parakeet.

"Wh-what's it doing back here? And what's that between its beak?" Sophia asked, shock reducing her voice to a whisper.

I looked on in disbelief at the black object clasped in the bird's mouth, realisation dawning on my face.

I felt bile rise in my throat. "Oh no! I think that's Mr Schimmel's ponytail!"

I forgot to warn poor old Mr Schimmel that we had left a savage, villainous bird in his sanctuary and now he was bird food.

Without waiting for a response, the bird gulped down what was left of Mr Schimmel and cocked its head sideways.

Chirp.

It flew off the mantelpiece, red eyes glowing with murderous intent as it readied itself to attack. My limbs were frozen in place. I knew this was the end.

Claws extended, beak growing unnaturally wide, the bird swooped across the room—

And was swallowed whole.

"Buster!" Sophia and I shouted together.

While I braced myself for the bird's attack, Buster had leapt from behind the sofa and gobbled up the parakeet, just as it was about to make me its dessert.

"You saved us you beautiful, smelly dog," Sophia said affectionately.

Buster stared intently at us. I never realised how piercing the dog's stare could be. For the first time since he turned up on our doorstep, I sensed something in those deep dark brown eyes... intelligence.

"Erm, Sophia? When did Buster first arrive on our

doorstep?" I asked, although I already knew the answer.

"Oh, I don't know... he was in the kitchen when I got home from school about seven or eight weeks ago—"

"About the same time the Caretaker appeared in school…"

And then, Buster opened his furry mouth and said, *"Finally, that chirping nuisance is gone, I've been waiting for a chance to finish it since it entered my new home."* The dog burped a yellow feather that floated into the air. *"Now – what does a pooch have to do to get fed around here?"*

THE END

Enjoy the first instalment of the terrifyingly-fun new **JITTERS** series?

Head on over to the author's website (www.LGCunningham.com) or Twitter page (@LG_Cunningham) to keep updated on future releases in the series... or to simply have a chat!

ABOUT THE AUTHOR

LG Cunningham loves to write scary, spine-chilling, monster filled, 'my-child-is-not-able-to-sleep' stories. This term of endearment could be as a result of growing up in an Irish town filled with ghosts, being able to communicate with (and actually see) the dead or more than likely because his family used to rent him horror movies (pre-Netflix and pre-DVDs) when he was very little which had the affect of twisting his brain to the extent that he was - and still is - afraid of his own shadow.

Printed in Great
Britain
by Amazon